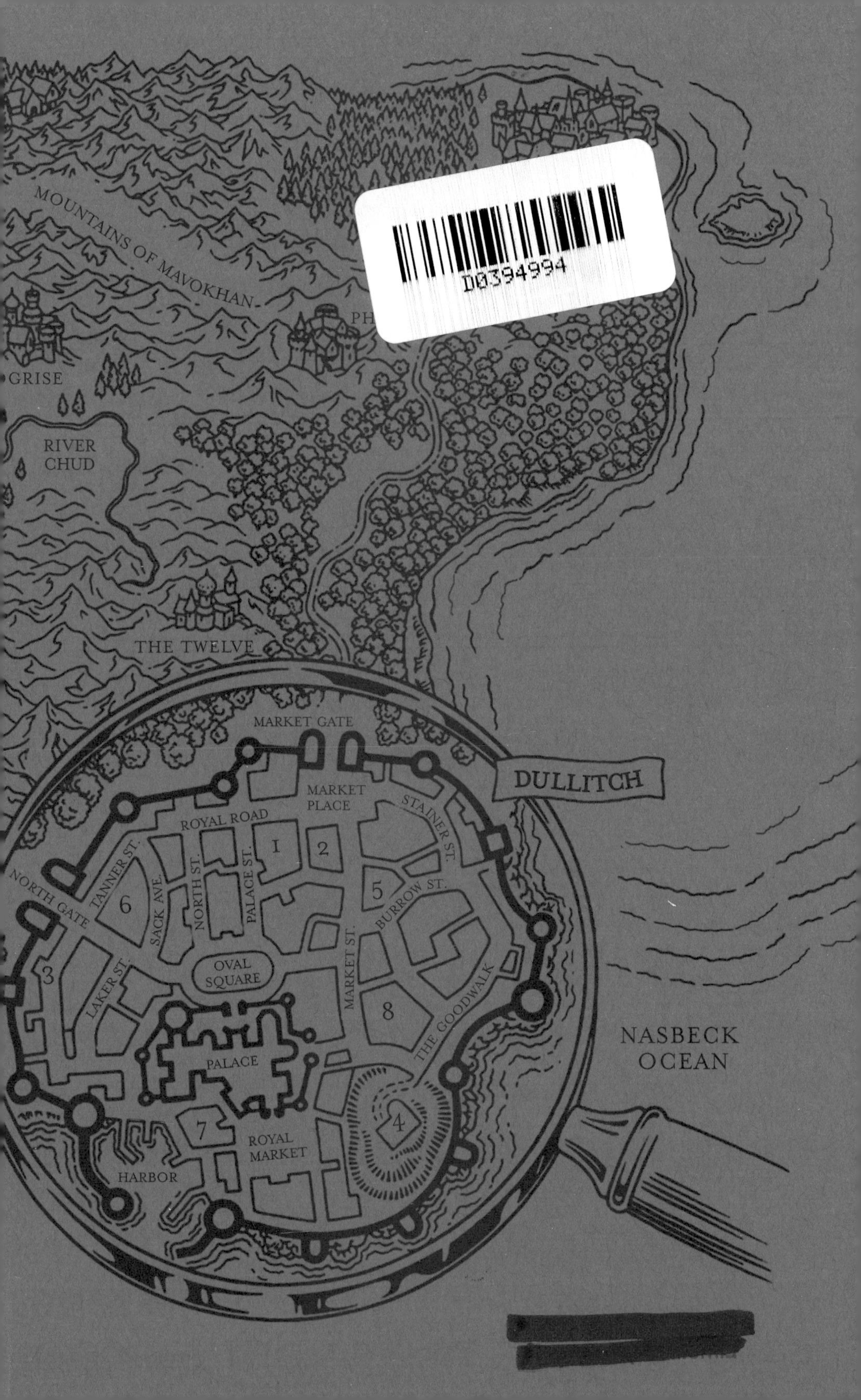
MOUNTAINS OF MAVOKHAN
GRISE
RIVER CHUD
THE TWELVE
MARKET GATE
DULLITCH
MARKET PLACE
ROYAL ROAD
STAINER ST.
1
2
TANNER ST.
NORTH ST.
PALACE ST.
5
BURROW ST.
NORTH GATE
6
SACK AVE.
MARKET ST.
OVAL SQUARE
3
LAKER ST.
THE GOODWALK
8
PALACE
NASBECK OCEAN
7
ROYAL MARKET
4
HARBOR

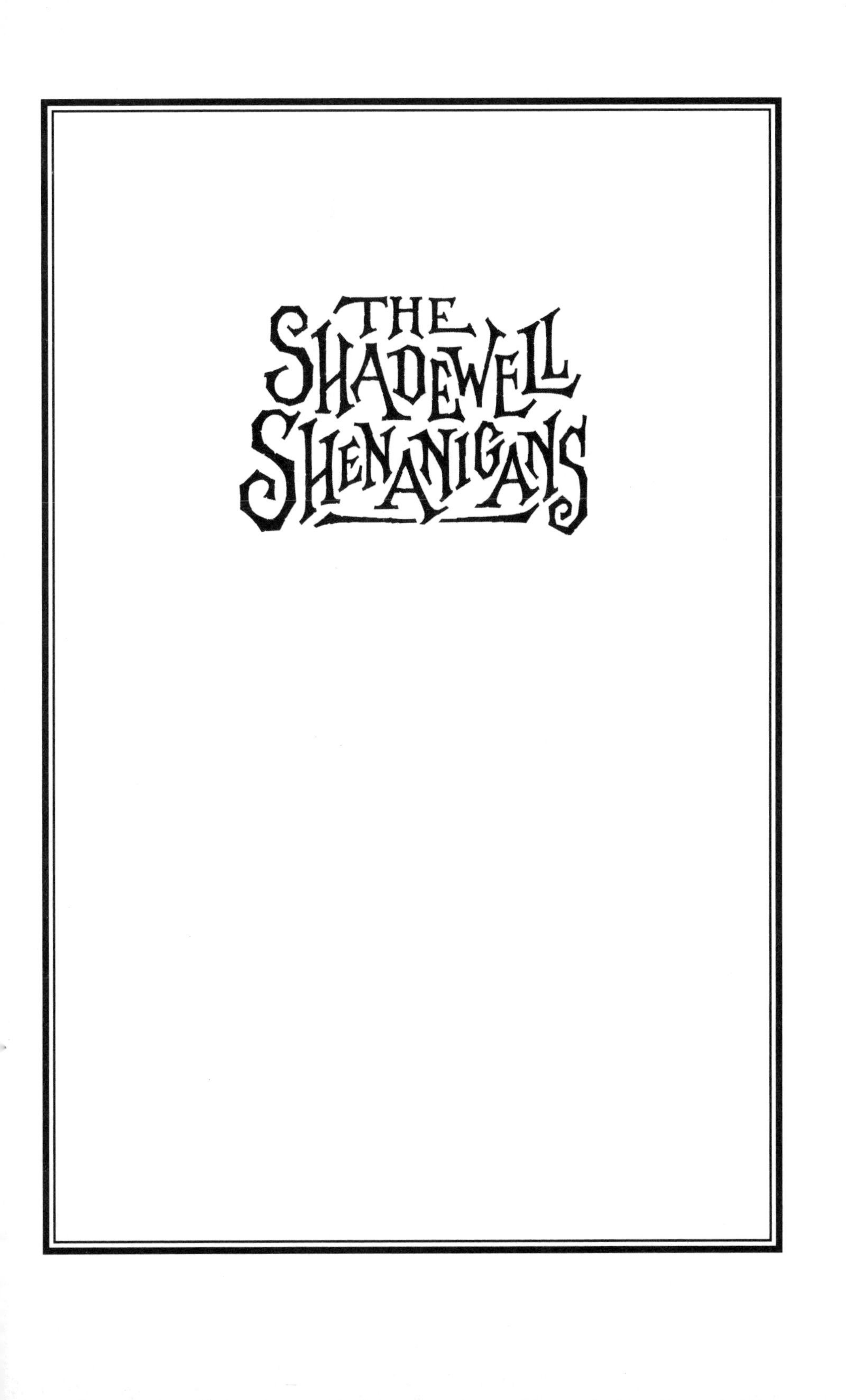
THE SHADEWELL SHENANIGANS

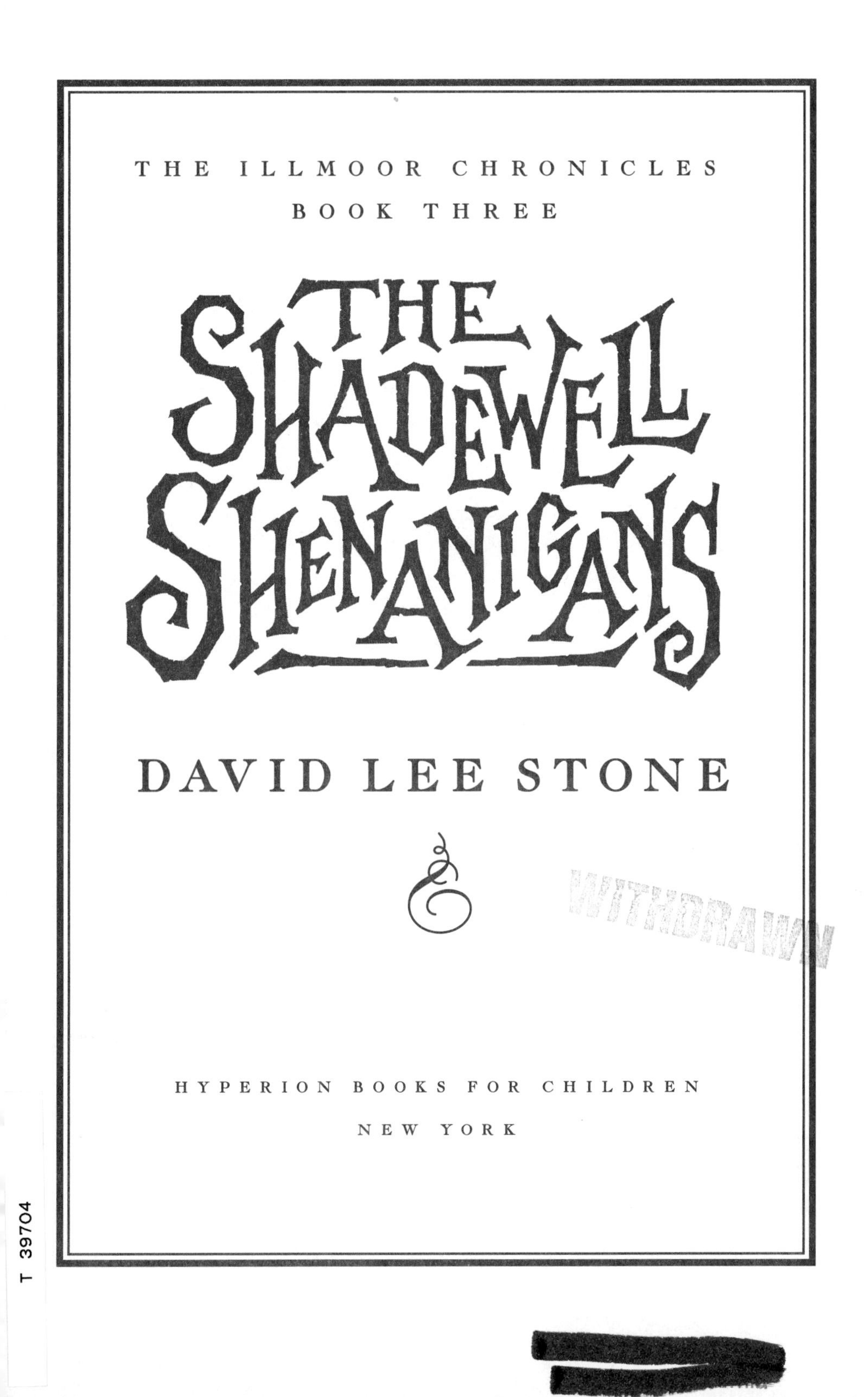

THE ILLMOOR CHRONICLES
BOOK THREE

THE SHADEWELL SHENANIGANS

DAVID LEE STONE

HYPERION BOOKS FOR CHILDREN
NEW YORK

Hyperion Books for Children,

114 Fifth Avenue, New York, New York 10011-5690.

First published in the U.K. by Hodder's Children's Books.

First U. S. edition, 2006.

1 3 5 7 9 10 8 6 4 2

Hand lettering by Leah Palmer Preiss

Printed in the United States of America

Reinforced binding

Library of Congress Cataloging-in-Publication Data on file.

ISBN 0-7868-3795-0

Visit www.hyperionbooksforchildren.com

For Chiara Louisa Tripodi,

my soulmate

SELECTED DRAMATIS PERSONAE

(ye cast of characters)

BIG, MR.: Gangster

BLOOD, PRINCE: Ruler of Legrash

CRAVEN, COUNT: Zombie warlord

CRIKEY, GENERAL: Phlegmian soldier

CURFEW, VISCOUNT: Ruler of Dullitch

GOLDEAXE, GORDO: Dwarf mercenary

KHAN, LADY: Wife of Count Craven

LAMBONTROFF, LOOGIE: Gangster

MARSHALL, PEGRAND: Manservant to Duke Modeset

MEDIOCRE, MR.: Gangster

MODESET, DUKE: Chairman of the Great Assembly

MUTTKNUCKLES, BARON: Ruler of Sneeze

PHEW, KING: Ruler of Phlegm

SALLOW, BRONWYN: Lady-in-waiting

STUMP: Wild adventurer or wildman

SUSTI, PRINCESS: Princess of Phlegm

TEETHGRIT, GAPE: Barbarian mercenary

TEETHGRIT, GROAN: Barbarian mercenary

TITCH, MR: Gangster

TUESDI, CUPPATEE: Goblin ring announcer

TWINLING, LOOGIE'S: Psychopathic demon

VICIOUS: Demented fox terrier

VISCERAL, EARL: Ruler of Spittle

PROLOGUE

THE MEETING took place in the village of Shadewell; a sure sign that something untoward was afoot.

Shadewell had a bad reputation, and not simply because it nestled beneath the western overhang of Shinbone Forest. The town, aside from being a haven for thieves and the more disreputable traders that frequented the southern shores, had played host to just about every major conspiracy in the history of Illmoor. In fact, no backstabbing murder plot was ever considered a threat until it could boast at least one high-level meeting in Shadewell. The villagers, who had a keen but necessarily detached interest in current affairs, occupied themselves during these anarchical gatherings by guessing who was going to be murdered next. Gold was seldom wagered on these guesses, though, because the process was so straightforward. All one needed to do in order to ascertain the presumed target was spot which great civic leader hadn't been invited to the table.

On this occasion, however, the villagers of Shadewell were left more than a little flummoxed; everyone who was anyone had turned up. Indeed, by lunchtime, all six permanent members of the Illmoorian Great Assembly had passed under the Shading Gate and into the village proper.

Viscount Curfew was the first to arrive. The ruling lord of Dullitch had left his entourage at the stables and had, to the great appreciation of the crowd, made his way to the village hall by foot, his long, dark cloak billowing out behind him like a possessed shroud.

Next to appear was Curfew's cousin, Duke Modeset, a notorious figure throughout Illmoor since his banishment from Dullitch following the hideous rat catastrophe. Modeset, much to the chagrin of his cousin, had been awarded the elevated position of Assembly Chairman, effectively allowing him a five-fingered veto throughout the proceedings. Curfew had only a one-fingered veto at *his* disposal, but it probably wasn't the sort he'd be allowed to use during a vote.

After Modeset, came King Phew of Phlegm, the richest member of the Great Assembly. He arrived in a golden carriage pulled by a pair of Chudderford Shires that were so incredibly intelligent, they'd waited until they'd been stabled before asking to use the toilet. Phew himself was a stout and sturdy man who attracted attention wherever he went, not merely due to his wealth, but because he walked while leaning backward: anyone who watched him was immediately put in mind of a limbo dancer, minus the bar.

The next arrival struck a stark contrast. Baron Muttknuckles, the regularly bankrupt and consistently violent lord of Sneeze, rolled up his sleeves at the door, elbowed his way into the village hall, and practically committed murder when the butler tried to take his deerskin coat. Eventually, after several arguments with fellow lords, the baron allowed the still-antlered beast to be removed, and blind eyes were turned as a full set of stolen crockery fell from one of the pockets.

Prince Blood, the premier of Legrash, arrived in a blaze of glory. Quite literally, in fact: his party had been attacked by Shinbone Footpads, who'd beaten up the prince's footmen and promptly set the royal carriage afire. As he arrived, several of his aides were trying to put him out and were beating him frantically about the head with a wet blanket, much to his apparent embarrassment.

Last to enter the village was the Earl of Visceral, the gaunt and angular primate of Spittle, who arrived complete with two skeletal bodyguards and, much to the amazement of the villagers, proceeded to dismantle them both and pack them away neatly in a small wooden suitcase before continuing to the hall.

Inside, the atmosphere was less than pleasant. Underneath a wide banner commemorating continental peace and the All-Cities Charter of 1014, several cries of "don't you threaten me" were quickly followed by a suggestion from Muttknuckles that Phew's incredibly muscular left arm had only become incredibly muscular since his wife had run off with her jester. Amid the tumult, Duke Modeset was in huddled conversation with Visceral, with whom he shared a great deal of common ground; partly because they had attended the same classes at Crestwell School, but mainly because he'd borrowed from the earl's land army in order to wrench the town of Fogrise back from a ferocious group of cardsharps.

"Can you believe this?" Curfew muttered to Blood. "How're we supposed to get anything done with such a row going on?"

"Oh, I expect it'll die down," said Blood, who'd been in attendance twice before and was thus a veteran of the proceedings. "It usually does."

"ORDER."

All eyes turned toward Pegrand Marshall, Modeset's faithful manservant, who'd brought a twenty-pound lumphammer to bear on the old oak table. The gesture was more ceremonial than aggressive, but it certainly got everyone's attention.

"Milord Modeset, in this, his most humbled and obsequious position, prays silence at this difficult time."

Modeset rolled his eyes, then reached up and pulled Pegrand's head level with his mouth.

"I've told you what to say, Pegrand," he whispered. "And I'd appreciate it if you didn't *add bits in*. It's bad enough not being able to address the assembly directly, without you making things worse."

His manservant nodded and returned his attention to the temporarily captivated audience.

"His lordship very much resents not being allowed to talk to you all personally," Pegrand continued, "and is somewhat surprised that he is still being treated like an exile in most parts of Illmoor, *despite* the fact that he saved the capital from a Yowler plot to destroy it. Still, as a once-disgraced noble, he is only permitted to chair the meeting, and not to address it. Therefore, I will be his voice for the duration of this meeting; a decision that has caused his lordship no small amount of stress. Does anybody have any objection to *my* addressing you all?"

There were a lot of shared glances and a few shrugs. Only Curfew nodded in agreement, but even *his* acknowledgement contained a reluctant edge.

Pegrand swallowed, progressing: "While I remember, Duke Modeset *does* wish to thank you for inviting him to chair this most vital of meetings . . . and he'd very much appreciate any donations you'd care to make toward the restoration of his ancestral home in Fogri—"

Without waiting for the speech to be concluded, Modeset leaped from his seat and snatched a handful of his servant's jerkin.

"Damn you, Pegrand! I told you to leave that bit until the end of the day. Now every one of them knows we're here with a begging bowl. Well, thank you. Thank you so very much."

He slumped back into the chair, folded his arms, and stared pointedly out of the window. His manservant went red in the face for a few moments, but proceeded.

"His, um, his lordship, er, I must apologize—I read that last bit wrong. His lordship is fine for money, and is doing very well for himself despite, erm, how things might look. In actual fact, we've both got new jerkins on order—"

"Shut up! Just shut up!" Modeset chimed in. "You're only making the situation worse! Just listen to yourself, man!"

Pegrand's frown was threatening to melt his face. "I'm sorry, milord, I really am! What should I say?"

"You think you're hard up?" Muttknuckles interjected. "I had to *walk* here."

"Excuse me, gentlemen," Curfew said, leaning across the table with a smile playing on his lips. "Much as I hate to interrupt this entertaining little pantomime, I would like to remind you that we are all here for a reason, and I, for one, cannot wait to get this discussion underway."

"Seconded," muttered Phew and Blood in unison.

Modeset shifted uncomfortably in his seat and, eventually, cleared his throat. "I know what the rules state," he began. "But may I at least be allowed to address the Assembly directly? After all, disgraced or not, I am supposed to be chairing this meeting."

"Aye."

"Very well."

"Get on with it, then."

The duke nodded, then leaned back in his seat and took a deep breath. "We are here today, gentlemen, to discuss a common threat." He waited for a murmur of agreement before continuing. "Each one of us has suffered untold humiliations at the hands of this menace, and not one of our beautiful cities has escaped his destructive attentions. Gentlemen, I think you will agree with me when I say that it is high time we rid ourselves of Groan Teethgrit."

The muttering around the table increased, but Modeset had regained the momentum and he wasn't about to let himself falter.

"I have here statements from your foreign ministers: one each from Spittle, Sneeze, Dullitch, and Legrash. Phlegm is a notable exception, but I'll come to that in a moment. For now, I would like to share with you a brief roundup of events involving this . . . continental landmass and his despicable associates."

Curfew sat up, Blood twitched, and even Muttknuckles was paying attention. The only people in the room not paying full heed to the duke's speech were Visceral, who'd helped to write it; and Phew, who was becoming increasingly nervous about his city being described as a "notable exception."

"Since Teethgrit and his midget partner escaped from Dullitch following my own exile," Modeset proceeded, staring pointedly at his cousin, "escaped, I might add, dressed as washerwomen. . . ."

Curfew glared at him.

"That is," Modeset plowed on, "a seven-foot, bald-headed washerwoman and her bearded, four-foot niece. . . ."

"Yes, yes! I think we've got the picture," Curfew snapped, ignoring the accusatory stares of his fellow leaders. "Do go on."

"Hmm . . . well, since that day, they have wreaked havoc across Illmoor, and I quote: 'seventy-two merchant caravans ambushed between Dullitch and Spittle, losing both cities somewhere in the region of fifty thousand crowns; the theft of countless bejeweled swords from the royal vault in Legrash, costing approximately thirty thousand crowns; and, more recently, several cases of arson and extraordinarily reckless vandalism in and around Sneeze, causing Baron Muttknuckles to slip even further into debt and depravity.' To date, only our Phlegmian cousins have escaped Teethgrit's ravenous hunger for chaos, but I assure you, Your Majesty, that even your fair city will not go unnoticed for long. I am now given to understand that these two unspeakably troublesome mercenaries have joined forces with the last surviving member of Teethgrit's tribal clan—a man, I might add, who boasts a list of criminal activities almost matching that of his half-wit brother—promising yet more mayhem and misery still to come." Modeset took a deep breath and shook his head disapprovingly. "The history books tell us that this one rogue tribe has terrorized our land for more than two centuries . . . and it falls to us—um—*you*, the five most powerful and influential leaders in Illmoor, to answer the question: why are you putting up with this? There're only two Teethgrits left, after all, and you do have four entire *armies* at your disposal. *And* Baron Muttknuckles."

Curfew was the first to respond. "Groan's worshipped as a hero in Dullitch," he said defensively. "Ever since he brought the children home under your own inimitable rule, he has been seen as the savior of the city."

"It's the same in Spittle," added Visceral. "News spreads quickly. D'you know, I went on an official visit to our oldest college last week, and the students actually had paintings of Groan Teethgrit over their beds!"

"My son has one," admitted Blood. "Lovely brushwork."

"Something must be done," Muttknuckles snapped. "But I'm telling you, I'd be mobbed if I sent my—um—guards after him. And as for the brother, well, we *tried* to arrest *him*, but he made mincemeat out of my best! I mean, he mailed my own captain back to me: I had to sign for the man! Now I've only got two soldiers left. My point is: we can't simply attack the Teethgrits, especially now that they're together."

"Har, har."

"Exactly," Curfew agreed. "We can't afford to send our own men after the Teethgrit band; and any lord who *does* manage to get Groan's blood on his hands is likely to be more despised by his people for shedding it!"

"Agreed! So what on Illmoor are we going to do?"

Modeset sat up slowly and grasped the arms of his chair.

"Gentlemen," he said. "I do have a plan. It's a long shot, but it might just work. It is certainly cunning enough, if played out correctly, to bring an end to Groan and his insolent little band—and without any *army* involvement to complicate things."

Silence. Nothing but silence, and some expectant faces.

"Like his barbarian brother," the duke announced, "Groan Teethgrit has two known weaknesses. First and foremost, the man simply cannot resist a challenge; and secondly, he *adores* beautiful women." Modeset turned to King Phew. "And that's where you come in."

"M-me?" exclaimed the Phlegmian monarch. "Wh-what can I do?"

Modeset smiled, produced a scroll from his jerkin, and smoothed it out on the great table.

"You can start by getting this poster seen by *certain* persons-at-large in or around your kingdom," he said. "It might take some time, but I'm quite sure we'll get the reaction we're looking for. . . ."

King Phew placed a finger on the corner of the

scroll and began to read, mumbling soundlessly. Then he sat back and swallowed several times, looking decidedly grim.

"What do you think?" Modeset asked as the scroll was passed around the table.

Phew blinked and cracked his knuckles. "I-I won't allow it."

Modeset's tiny eyes narrowed to slits. "*You* won't allow it?" he repeated slowly.

"I—" Phew began, his voice uneasy. "That is, *she'll* never agree to it, never in a million years."

Modeset shuffled his chair over to the old man and snaked a greasy arm around him.

"She doesn't have to know," he whispered.

When Phew looked up again, every eye in the room was staring at him expectantly.

PART ONE

THE CHALLENGE

ONE

A CROWD of more than four hundred visitors had gathered in Bludly Wood for the last day of "The Limbbreaker," an annual wrestling tournament that was quickly becoming one of Western Illmoor's largest tourist attractions.

A weighing system comprising two enormous cages had been rigged up on a hastily assembled scaffold, one containing a multitude of tiny green creatures, and one half open for the use of a grizzly queue of potential combatants.

Three lines of thick hemp rope had been draped among four trees to form a square of combat, and an impossibly tall elf had stepped between them in order—the crowd assumed—to make some sort of announcement. However, when a statement was finally issued, it came not from the elf, but from a tiny goblin perched jauntily on the elf's left shoulder. The goblin was carrying a twisty loudspeaker.

"Ladies and gentlemen, boys and girls, welcome back to the last day of the Limbbreaaaaakkaaar tournament! I am your host, Cuppatee Tuesdi, and *this* is our closing contest, scheduled for *one* fall, a submission, or a knockout. I invite you to take a quick look at the progress of our two finalists. . . ."

The goblin indicated, and all eyes turned away from the ring to consider an enormous chalkboard nailed to the nearest oak. It read:

QUARTER FINALS

Big "Nige" Trollsort vs. Mad Mick "The Ogre"

Winner: Double Disqualification

Groan Teethgrit vs. Ruby Twoshoes

Winner: Groan Teethgrit

(opponent disqualified for being a woman in disguise)

Grid Thungus vs. The Mighty Minter

Winner: Double Countout

Gape Teethgrit vs. "Muscles" Mirko

Winner: Gape Teethgrit

SEMIFINALS

Groan Teethgrit vs. (vacant)

(vacant) vs. Gape Teethgrit

FINAL

Groan Teethgrit vs. Gape Teethgrit

The goblin continued: "Coming down the aisle, weighing in at two hundred and ninety-six twadlings and hailing from the Mountains of Mavokhan, I give you GAAAAAPE TEEEEETHGRITTTTAHHH!"

The crowd divided like an enchanted sea to admit the imposing form of Gape Teethgrit, who pounded down the aisle like a man possessed, leaping over the ropes and landing, one successful somersault later, squarely on his feet. While the crowd jeered wildly at the warrior, he secured his long hair in a ponytail and made sure his ankle guards were tightly locked.

"Annnnnd his opponent," the goblin continued warbling into the speaker, "accompanied to the square by his manager, Gordo Goldeaxe, weighing in at three hundred and six twadlings, and also from the Mountains of Mavokhan, GROOOAAAANN TEEEETHGRITTT!"

A cheer exploded from the crowd as they parted once again to reveal Gape's half brother. The larger of the two barbarians plodded down the aisle, stepped straight between the ropes, and slugged his sibling hard in the face. As Gape crashed to the floor, a small but sturdy-looking dwarf hurried to the side of the square and began to bark orders.

Gordo Goldeaxe looked nervous. It had taken him the best part of a week to persuade the brothers to enter the competition, and he was already regretting the effort. He beckoned Groan over to him and, when the barbarian finally hulked across the ring and leaned down, whispered: "What did you hit him for? We're faking this, remember?"

Groan frowned. "I 'it all the uvvers."

"Yes, I *know*! *That's* because they were bloody strangers: we've got a *scam* going. If this fight's a tie, then we get *both* lots of money, plus a bonus from the ring crew, because all the visitors will come back next year to see who wins out. That's *fifty* crowns for Gape, twenty for you, and thirty for me. Remember how I told you to work it out?"

"Yeah," said Groan doubtfully, "but I don't see no 'arm in 'ittin' 'im."

"Fake it!"

"Why?"

Gordo sighed in exasperation. "He's your brother, for cryin' out loud!"

"So? I don' like 'im."

"Neither do I! But you wanted this all along. And besides, think of the *money*."

"What money?"

The dwarf was about to go through the whole plan again, when Groan was suddenly taken off his feet by a ferocious leg-sweep.

The big barbarian landed on his back, moaned a bit, and then rolled over and grabbed a tree in order to regain his stance.

Gordo scowled at Gape's victorious grin, then shielded his eyes as Groan muscled up and hit the barbarian with a head-butt that could probably have been heard in Spittle. Gape tumbled backward, swung on the ropes, and quickly retaliated with a reverse hamster-kick. The crowd roared their approval.

Quick to capitalize on the move, Gape hurried around the back of the ring and seized his brother in a vicious chiselfoot-leg-vise. The crowd was about to applaud again, when Groan broke out.

The giant barbarian lumbered to his feet, blocked two right-handers, and snatched his brother by the hair. Then he drove his head under Gape's chin and dropped onto his knees, delivering a jawbuster that sent shudders through the sympathetic audience. He quickly followed up the move with two full blacksmiths and a half roadsweeper.

By this point, Gordo had his eyes shut and his stubby hands clamped tightly over his ears (a precautionary gesture that did little to prevent him feeling every crack and thud as various blows were executed).

The action in the ring was heating up.

Gape catapulted himself from the ropes toward his brother. Groan ducked, and they caught each other with a vicious washing-line maneuver, leaving them both down for the count.

The elf with the shoulder-goblin, who'd been circling since the two warriors had entered the ring, suddenly dropped to its knees and began to pound the ground. The goblin announced its actions to the crowd.

One.

"ONE!"

Two.

"TWO!"

Three.

"THREE!"

A group of official soldiers from Phlegm had been mingling in the crowd, and one of them pushed past Gordo, thrusting a small poster of some kind into the dwarf's hands. Gordo's attention shifted briefly from the match as he watched the soldiers continue to make their way through the crowd. Eventually, when it became obvious that the group had moved on, he returned his focus to the fight.

Eight.

"EIGHT!"

Nine.

"NINE!"

Ten.

"TEN! A TIE! THE CONTEST IS A TIE!"

The crowd booed, hissed, and began to shuffle away to the various food stalls surrounding the area. Groan and Gape lay still for a further five minutes as per their instructions, and Gordo, well pleased with himself as he noticed the treasurer counting out a generous stack of gold, unfurled the parchment that had been handed to him and read:

WANTED:

MAN TO MARRY

THE RICHEST PRINCESS IN ILLMOOR.

APPLICANTS MUST BE OVER SEVEN FEET TALL

AND MUSCULAR WITH NICE TEETH AND

CONSIDERABLE SKILL WITH A SWORD.

ACCEPTABLE CANDIDATES GET
A ONE-DAY TRIAL PERIOD EACH,
FOLLOWED BY A CHANCE TO COMPETE IN THE
ARENA FOR THE LADY'S FAIR HAND!
APPLY TO: PRINCESS SUSTI,
PHLEGM KEEP, PHLEGM

Gordo sniggered at the advertisement, reflected that the princess in question had to be a complete moose, and tossed the scroll away. Groan caught it.

"Wass this?" he boomed, his brother striding up behind him.

"It's nothing," Gordo assured them both, snatching Gape's arm and hurrying the younger barbarian over to the treasurer's table.

Groan frowned as he attempted to make sense of the words; reading had never been one of his strong points. After his third attempt had got him as far as "Wanted," he called to one of the scantily clad dancing girls who had accompanied him to the ring during the earlier rounds. She hurried over.

"You know words?" Groan asked.

"Yes, Mr. Teeth. I can speak Illmoor, Goblin, and Orcish."

"Read this for me, p'ease."

"Certainly, Mr. Teeth."

Gordo had managed to extract a hundred crowns from the tournament's treasurer; his day was only slightly marred when Gape decided he wouldn't accept his share.

"What'd you mean, 'that's not enough'?" he snapped as the barbarian slowly shook his head.

"I mean exactly what I said, Gordo. You've given me forty-eight crowns; the agreement was for FIFTY."

Gordo sighed and slapped two more crowns into the warrior's open palm. "Just remember that *we're* allowing *you* to join *us*, not the other way 'round."

Gape nodded and leaned close to the dwarf. "And just you remember which brother you're dealing with," he snarled. "Groan and I may share the same father, but the similarity ends there."

Gordo sneered at the warrior, failed to shove him aside, and waddled around him instead. When he'd made his way back to where Groan was standing, he was shocked to see the barbarian deep in conversation with one of the Phlegmian soldiers. The man was showing Groan a scrolled painting of some kind.

"What's going on here?" Gordo asked, glaring at

the soldier with barely disguised malice. "I'm only away five minutes and you're already mixing with the *enemy*."

"I ain't mixin'," Groan bellowed, turning the scroll around so that Gordo could get a good look at it. "I'm in love."

"Who's that?"

"*That*," intoned the solider, "is Her Royal Highness, the Princess of Phlegm."

Gordo shrugged. "She's nothing special."

"Are you joking?" Groan exclaimed. "She's the bes' lookin' woman I ever saw!"

"Get out of it; my mother's prettier than her."

"Your muvver's bald."

"Yeah, *and*?"

Gordo shook his head in disbelief. "You're actually considering it, aren't you?" he said. "You really think that girl'd look at you twice?"

"Not once she's seen *me*," said a voice, and Gape snatched the scroll from Groan's fumbling fingers. "Felicsataris Trumidia, a woman of unspeakable beauty."

"Oi!" Groan echoed. "Stuff off out o' it; I saw her first."

"Yes, well you'd *have* to, because if she saw you

first, she'd run a two-minute mile. Ha-ha-ha-ha!"

The soldier, who'd been grinning slyly ever since the girl had led Groan over to him, cleared his throat. "I know," he said. "Why don't you *both* apply? That way, I can arrange for you each to spend a day with the princess before the list of applicants becomes too . . . crowded." He glanced down at Gordo. "You can bring your gnome, by all means."

"I'm a dwarf!" Gordo snapped. "And I'll bring my bloody self, if I've a mind to."

"I should hurry, if I were you," the solider concluded, calling over one of his subordinates and politely reclaiming the portrait from Gape. "After all, opportunities such as this seldom come along every day."

TWO

"NEWS, MILORD!"

The drafty corridors of Phlegm Keep's east wing echoed as Pegrand hurried along, stopping at each gloomy portal in an effort to locate the duke. They'd been secret guests of King Phew's ever since the meeting in Shadewell, in order to "insure" that the plan proceeded smoothly.

Pegrand soldiered on. He eventually found Modeset in a small chapel behind the library, tossing scraps to his insane terrier. The dog in question, whose name (as well as its nature) was Vicious, looked as if it would happily rip the duke's throat out but couldn't be bothered to muster the effort. Pegrand steered well clear of it.

"News, milord!"

Modeset didn't take his eyes off the dog, but

nodded slowly. "Did you know, Pegrand," he began, "that this keep has a shark-infested moat?"

"Er, no, milord, but—"

"Isn't that wonderful? I swam with sharks when I was a boy, you know. My father's lagoon was full of them: he used to drop me in it from time to time—"

The manservant gasped. "What? You mean, on purpose?"

"Oh, he was only messing about." Modeset chuckled. "He loved me, really, it was just his way. Funny thing was, I'd be swimming around for hours, and none of the sharks ever went for me. I can just see my father's face now, screwed up in disbelief, when I casually climbed out after a good afternoon's breaststroke. Now, you were saying?"

"Milord?" Pegrand took a moment to compose himself. "There's some important news," he said.

"Yes, I *had* gathered that. What type of news, exactly?"

"Well—"

"You know that if it's bad news, I don't want it. . . ."

"Yes, milord."

"I'm serious, Pegrand. One more 'unfortunately,' and you're fired."

"Right—"

"Please take that threat to include all *I regret to inform you*'s and *you're not going to believe this*'s. Are we clear?"

The manservant rolled his eyes and nodded. "*Yes*, milord, but it's *good* news."

"Very well. If you'll wait for just one moment. . . ."

Modeset turned his head slightly, eyes still fixed on the dog. Then he took two deep breaths and lunged sideways, snatching the animal up by the scruff of its neck mere seconds before it exploded in a fit of gnashing teeth and flying spit.

Motioning for his servant to open a large cage at the far end of the chapel, Modeset crossed the floor, struggling to keep hold of the raging fur ball, and deposited his pet in its holding pen, slamming the door shut and clicking a fat padlock over the bars. Then he wrapped a tissue around his bleeding arm and collapsed into a nearby pew.

"Pegrand, you may begin."

The manservant paused for a moment before mumbling: "You know, I think I've forgotten what it was, now. . . ."

"Get *on with it*!"

"Yes, milord; just a little joke, there. Um . . .

we've had a message from King Phew. He says that Groan Teethgrit and his brother have swallowed the bait."

Modeset raised an eyebrow, his lips on the brink of a smile. "They've both applied to meet the princess?" he hazarded.

"Yes, milord. Apparently, they're both on the way to Phlegm."

"Alone?"

"Well, yes, milord, apart from the dwarf."

Modeset nodded. "We always knew he'd be part of the equation. King Phew has made all the . . . preparations?"

"Yes, milord. His herald says both men will be well entertained, and each'll be given a day to spend in the princess's company. Then they'll go to the arena to see which one gets to propose."

"All as it should be," said Modeset, tucking in the edge of his impromptu bandage.

Pegrand hesitated in the doorway, looking momentarily doubtful. "What if they kill each other, milord?"

"A bonus," said Modeset quickly.

"And if they don't?"

"If they don't, Pegrand, then good King Phew

can begin to put the rest of my ingenious plan into action. Now, be so kind as to fetch dinner."

"Er . . . yes, right away, milord. I'm afraid it's grit 'n' pebble soup again, though. They seem to go in for that a lot here."

Modeset let out a deep and painful breath. "If there's nothing else, Pegrand," he sighed, "I'll be in the archivist's suite, reminiscing about better times."

Pegrand nodded. "I get the hint, milord. Dinner won't be long."

There came a small, embarrassed knock on the door of the Phelgmian archives.

The custodian of the archives, an ancient man in full possession of his considerable faculties, looked up from a dusty, leather-bound tome and wondered whether he'd imagined the sound. After all, no one had visited the archives in what seemed like an age.

Silence. Then, again: *knock, knock*.

The archivist rummaged around on the table for his spectacles and, upon locating them, struggled to his feet.

"Come in?" he called.

The door opened a fraction, and Duke Modeset stuck his head through the gap. "Excuse me, but I wondered whether I might trouble you for a moment."

The archivist nodded his head, discharging a torrential mixture of dust and dandruff. "Of course, of course!" he spluttered. "The archives are free for everyone to enjoy. Please, be my guest."

Modeset nodded and slipped through the door, pushing it closed behind him. The room was filled from floor to ceiling with books, and when the elderly archivist motioned for his guest to occupy a seat, it took the duke five minutes to identify one. Eventually, he brushed a pile of scrolls from a suitable-looking stool, and took his rest.

"Now," the archivist began, peering at Modeset over the top of his spectacles, "what exactly are you looking for?"

The duke hesitated for a moment, then smiled. "I understand you have records here for Crestwell."

The archivist clapped his hands. "Of course! We have details of every priest to have served under—"

Modeset shook his head. "Not the cathedral," he said. "The *school*."

There was a moment of stony silence.

"I'm afraid I'm not at liberty to disclose that information to anyone except select members of the nobility."

"I am Duke Modeset, Lord of Fogrise and former ruler of Dullitch and its environs."

The archivist looked suddenly flustered. "Oh, I'm so sorry, milord! I didn't recognize—that is, I'm afraid that I don't see very well these days."

"Never mind," Modeset said. "But if I may—"

"Of course! Um . . . I need to, that is, could I possibly examine your seal?"

Modeset nodded, producing his hallmark from a breast pocket and proffering it to the old man for closer inspection. The archivist eventually handed it back and began to waddle over toward one of the giant volume stacks in the far corner of the room.

"An old pupil, lordship?" he muttered, lifting the top three books and placing them on the floor beside the pile.

"Yes," Modeset muttered. "Unfortunately, I am."

The archivist chuckled. "All the great families were," he said. "That's the thing about Crestwell, isn't it? Its famous pupils divide neatly into the great and the terrible of today."

Modeset made an uncomprehending face

behind the old man, but said nothing.

"What year?" the archivist asked, narrowing his stack pile down to eight grubby books.

"Nine hundred and eighty-five."

"House?"

"Razors."

"Oh, dear me, really?"

Modeset ignored the archivist's sudden intake of breath, and nodded.

"Yes, *really*."

"Very well, then. Here it is! The notes below each name are mine. You understand: I do so like to keep things up to date."

The archivist tottered back to the duke and deposited a heavy book in his lap. It was open at the correct page.

Modeset allowed himself a smile as his gaze spilled over the text:

CRESTWELL SENIORS:
LEAVING YEAR 985 HOUSE OF RAZORS

OZRYK, SHELMETH
[became Earl of Beanstalk 991, died, 993 (poisoning)]

CURFEW, RAVIS
[heir to the throne of Dullitch, ascended following

Duke Modeset's expulsion from the city, 1002.]

SAPP, VADNEY
[heir to the throne of Crust, disappeared in mysterious circumstances, 995]

DIVEAL, SORRY
[trained as a sorcerer in Shinbone, then went bad and tried to destroy the town: fled when reinforcements arrived from Crust. Disappeared, 1001]

VISCERAL, VORTAIN
[trained as a sorcerer in Shinbone, then ascended to the throne in Spittle, 990; found religion and helped to banish sorcery as a legal pursuit in Illmoor]

BLOOD, VIKTARR
[crown prince of Legrash, took the throne shortly after leaving Crestwell, 986]

MUTTKNUCKLES, JIVE
[heir to the Barony of Sneeze. Left Crestwell, then ran away when his father died, in 987, and had to be dragged back and chained to the throne in order to rule. Has enjoyed a reluctant (but peaceful) reign]

Modeset swallowed as his eyes found the last entry on the page:

MODESET, VANDRE
[heir to the throne of Dullitch, ascended to rule the

capital in 986, following the death of Duke Edwyn Vitkins (uncle), but was firmly ejected during the infamous "rat catastrophe" in 1002. Currently in disgrace, though rumored to be a sure bet for the "complimentary" chair of the Great Assembly. Owns an ancestral home in the district of Fogrise, but remains the only living lord without a city.]

Modeset read the last line through twice before slamming the book shut, his eyes welling up as the truth of the statement bit into his soul. *The only living lord without a city*. How had it come to this?

Modeset shut his eyes, ignoring the archivist's incessant chatter, and tried to focus on the positives. As far as he could determine, he had three things going for him: a loyal manservant, a plan to rid the continent of an unwanted menace, and . . . and . . . and a healthy dog. The rest would come. He *would* rule again. As his father so often used to say, an opportunity would present itself. . . .

THREE

SEVERAL WEEKS later, in Phlegm's giant arena, two swords clashed in the air. There followed a brief yelp before a goblin head flew wide and bounced along the ground several times, rolling to a halt.

A cheer erupted from the crowd.

Gordo Goldeaxe leaped onto a rock and took a moment to review the situation. There were ten goblins decapitated, six red ogres in the scorpion pit, and it looked as though Groan had the king's elephantine moon troll on the run. That was the good news: the bad news was that, over on the opposite side of the arena, Gape Teethgrit and his magically accurate blades were doing just as well. In fact, not only had Groan's half brother made light work of the goblins *and* the red ogres, he'd also persuaded *his* moon troll to break its chains in a dramatic bid for freedom. Predictably, King Phew had both creatures shot before they reached the arena doors.

Gordo sighed: it was going to be another tie. How much longer could they go on like this?

"Done 'im," roared Groan Teethgrit, swaggering up with an air of arrogance peculiar to the barbarian class. "Where'd them goblins go?"

"I've killed them all," Gordo admitted, indicating the pile of bodies around his rock. "And before you ask, no, I haven't scalped you any hair."

"I'll get an 'an'ful, meself."

"Forget the wig, Groan; smooth's a good look for you." The dwarf grinned encouragingly. Then he jumped down off the rock and removed the cracked iron helmet that had practically been hammered into his skull by goblin blades. "I see your brother's doing well."

Groan peered across the arena floor, and cursed. " 'ginner's luck," he said.

"I doubt that," Gordo replied, rapping on the helmet to see if he needed a new one. "Let's face it, Groan, he's every bit the warrior you are, and those swords of his are more than a match for both our weapons combined. They *hum*, Groan. You don't even see the damn things until they're sticking in your chest!"

"Yeah," Groan agreed thoughtfully. "Maybe you should fight wiv 'im for a bit; give me a chance."

"I'll ignore that," Gordo said, drawing in a long breath. "Still, it's a pity it's come to this. You two used to get on fine before . . . well, you know. Women, eh? More trouble than they're worth. I reckon you should just let this one go. . . ."

"No way."

Groan flexed his jostling muscles and straightened up. At seven feet tall, he was a sight to behold. Then again, Gordo reflected, so was his half brother. In fact, the only noticeable physical difference between them, apart from an inch or two of height, was Groan's inordinate lack of hair and his brother's profuse abundance of it. Mentally, however, they were a world apart.

The dwarf finished toying with his helmet and discarded it. Then he raised his stout battle-axe to signal to the royal audience that their fight was over.

The distant shape of King Phew, High Lord of Phlegm, got to its feet and began to applaud. The rest of the crowd soon joined in, but a second burst of applause announced an even greater victory for the junior Teethgrit. To the delight of the crowd, Gape had stacked all the ogre arms in an amusing pyramid and was bowling a goblin skull at them.

"Pathetic," Gordo grumbled. "Absolutely pathetic. Look at him parading up and down as if he's the Duke of Dullitch. Makes me sick."

Groan nodded his head to one side. "I don't reckon' they should let 'im 'ave them swords."

"Oh, don't be an idiot!" Gordo muttered, beginning the long walk back to the podium. "If they ban his swords from the arena, then they'd sure as hell ban *me*. In fact, while we're on the subject, I don't even know what I'm doing here; remind me again?"

"Friendship," Groan barked. "'Sides, I came wiv you when you went to fight that bloke what took all them kiddies outta Dullitch."

Gordo rounded on his friend like an angry dog. "Ha! You were in that for the gold, Groan Teethgrit. Don't even try to deny it."

"Yeah, well, you're probably in this for the, for the, for the, for the—"

"Goblin snot?"

"No, I was gonna say 'fun.'"

"Fun? Fun?! You've got to be joking. What's fun about wrestling slaves, killing ogres, and jumping giant mantraps?"

Groan shrugged. "'S a laugh, innit?" he said. "You know, 'venture in forgotten lands an' all."

"Forgotten lands?" Gordo boggled at him. "We're in Phlegm."

"Yeah, well. You know what I mean."

Gordo came to a sudden halt, so sudden in fact that Groan almost walked right over him.

"Listen," the dwarf began, stepping back from his partner and raising an eyebrow, "is she really worth all this?"

"How d'you mean?"

"It's simple. I'm asking you if, after a single date, you can be truly, head over heels, one hundred percent in love with this princess?"

"Yeah, I am."

Gordo heaved a sigh. "What is it about her that makes you so sure that she's the one?"

The barbarian scratched his scalp. Groan had been completely bald ever since a battle with a sewer dragon some eight years ago, when a ball of flame had singed his crew cut. Curiously, the hair had never grown back.

"I love 'er wiv all my 'eart," he said eventually. "She's my ol' mate."

"I think you mean 'soul mate,'" Gordo corrected him. "And I seem to recall your saying much the same thing about Sue Ellen of Trumpinit."

"Yeah, I loved 'er, too."

"Well, she didn't love you."

"She did 'n' all."

"No, she didn't, Groan. She tried to kill you, remember?"

"She never."

"She did so!"

"No! I was just clumsy that mornin'. I fell."

"Down seven flights? She'd greased every damn step, Groan. Are you really that stupid?"

The barbarian tightened his jaw, then straightened up and turned away from his friend.

"Do what you like," he muttered. "I'm gonna get me a wife."

"Fine," Gordo snapped, driving his axe into the rough sand of the arena floor. "Just don't come to me when it all ends in tears . . . or when Gape beats you in the next trial."

"Nobody beats Groan Teethgrit," the barbarian called back. "I'm my own worst enemy, I am."

Gordo rolled his eyes. "That doesn't mean what you think it means!" he yelled.

Phlegm Keep basked in the heat of the generous Illmoor sun. It was a busy place at the best of times, an unfortunate consequence of being home to the richest family in all of Illmoor, but today the corridors were positively seething with activity. Nowhere was this more apparent than in the main courtyard of the keep, where most of the townsfolk had gathered to hear the latest installment of the princess's sensational love triangle. One of the barbarians had already arrived back from the arena; the crowd was anxiously anticipating the arrival of the other. They didn't have long to wait.

Gape Teethgrit strode into the courtyard of Phlegm Castle, sheathed both his swords, and yawned loudly.

"How's it going?" he asked Groan, who was standing in a widening circle in the center of the square, staring up at the royal balcony.

Groan shrugged and folded his muscular arms.

"Not talking, eh? Can't say I blame you; nobody likes a thrashing."

If the barbarian was rankled by this, he wasn't letting it show.

"Of course," Gape went on, "we both know who won. I mean, it might be a tie on *paper*, but we both know who's got the mustard for this particular caper. So, if I may be so bold"—he paused at this point to secure his jet locks in a tight ponytail—"why don't you pack up your great big sword and all your little daggers, grab that dwarf of yours, and sod off?"

Groan turned his head very slightly. "You talk a lot o' damn rubbish, Gape Teethgrit. Anyone ever tell you that?"

"Ha! Rubbish, eh? You'll be playing a new tune on your mouthpiece come morningtide! Ha-ha-ha-ha—"

The barbarian's derisory laughter was cut off by the fanfare that erupted from the balcony above. Several members of the royal family had stepped into view. They included King Phew and the delectable but reticent Princess Susti.

The king held up a hand for silence. "My daughter wishes to make an announcement."

The crowd held their breath, though there were a few extra gasps as Gordo shouldered his way through the bustle to second his ungrateful partner.

"First things first," the king droned on, his dull monotone almost counteracting the audience's enthusiasm for the news. "I must find out if our competitors' love for my daughter is strong, bold, and true . . . and I'm asking, you, Number Two, is this so?"

Groan hesitated for a moment, partly because he was still working out the question and partly because he couldn't remember what number he'd been given. Eventually, he managed to solve the enigma using the process of elimination: Gape was number one. This, coupled with the fact that Gordo was holding up two fingers, gave the whole game away.

"I do," Groan thundered, provoking a succession of nervous laughter from the crowd, and some not-so-nervous laughter from Gape, who leaned closer to his rival and whispered, "I hope for your sake the questions don't get any harder."

Before Groan could reply, King Phew shouted, "And you, Number One, you feel the same way?"

Gape gave an exaggerated nod. "She is my *reason*, Majesty," he cried.

"Very well." The king bowed his head. "My daughter, who as many of you will know, is against cruelty to the lower breeds, demands that there be no further trials in the arena."

The crowd began to mutter among themselves.

"Therefore, she has suggested an alternative challenge."

Gordo's bushy brows furrowed with suspicion.

"What has Her Royal Highness decided?" Gape yelled, wincing slightly as Groan began to grind his teeth.

The king stepped aside graciously, and his daughter replaced him at the front of the balcony.

"When I was young," she began, turning her sparkling blue eyes on the two barbarians, "I was told by my mother that the qualities a princess truly requires in her prince are a strong heart, a measure of courage, and a fathomless depth of devotion. Now, I can attest, having spent considerable time with both of these men, that a strong heart is not in question here. My warrior Gape treated me to a wonderful dinner at The Grand Hall, followed by a romantic boat ride through Cast Lake, and a moonlight serenade on his infamous pipes. My warrior Groan was kind enough . . . to give me one of his late father's teeth. Both acts prove a worthy heart."

Gordo winced and glanced up at Groan, who was grinning proudly.

"As for courage," the princess went on, "both men have proved themselves in the arena. So now we come to devotion . . . and devotion will settle it. Before I bestow my hand in marriage, I shall require—"

The entire audience held their breath: townsfolk, barbarians, visitors, clerks, guards, and the remainder of the royal family (who were more than a little annoyed that they'd not been given a proof copy of the speech).

Susti took a deep breath and continued: ". . . Something Old, Something New, Something Borrowed, and Something Blue."

The crowd gave a collective sigh. There were several mutterings along the lines of "big deal," "easy peasy," and "what a letdown."

Then Susti opened a scroll, and every eye in the courtyard was focused on her once again.

"For the Something Old, I would like the Idol of Needs, which, legend tells us, was buried beneath a Y-shaped tree on the distant Island of Kazbrack."

Gape's face dropped like a stone down a well. Even Groan looked momentarily put out.

"That's more 'an a day away," he rumbled, glaring up at the king. "What's she want that for?"

"I need it to prove your love," Susti exclaimed, her voice suddenly tense.

Gape Teethgrit, usually the first to accept a challenge, puffed out his cheeks and began to initialize some strange neck exercises. Gordo suspected that he was surreptitiously looking for the exit.

An uneasy silence descended on the courtyard. At the back of the crowd, an old man was employing a series of spasmodic hand gestures in order to take bets on who'd be the first through the gates. He was still working out the odds when a voice boomed:

"I'LL DO IT."

Gape shook himself from his reverie just in time to see the crowd's explosive reaction to Groan's statement. Gordo Goldeaxe was shaking his head emphatically, but the giant barbarian had already raised his hand for more silence.

"I'LL GO TO KUDBRICK!"

"Kazbrack," the king interrupted.

"YEAH, THASSIT, AND I'LL BRING BACK THE IDOL I NEEDS."

"*Of* Needs, Groan: the Idol *of* Needs."

"YEAH, WHATEVER. I'LL BRING THAT BACK AS WELL."

"Ha!" cried Gape, stepping up to his half brother and facing him, nose to nose. "Well, not if I get there first!"

"Break it up, break it up!" Gordo waded in between the two waists and managed to shove the warring brothers apart. "I have a question myself!"

Susti peered down at the dwarf. "What is your question, little warrior?"

Gordo muttered something under his breath, but carefully concealed his annoyance with a smile. "I was just wondering, Your Majesty—"

"Yes?"

"Well, you said you wanted four things, didn't you? Something Old, Something New, Something Borrowed, and Something Blue? So, what are the other three?"

The silence was actually tangible now; people were cutting it up at the back of the room and selling it.

"You are correct, little friend," Susti conceded, ignoring Gordo's pained expression and rolling eyes. "And so I must continue. For the Something New, I really had my heart set on Ezra's Opal."

"You what?" Groan yelled, suddenly forgetting himself. The crowd didn't really notice; they were glued to the princess's lips, anticipating the next shock announcement.

"Ezra's Opal," the princess repeated. "It's a

priceless stone set in a golden ring, fashioned by the demon miners of the Gleaming Mountains, and given to Lady Khan by her husband."

There was some hushed mumbling.

"Erm . . . I'm sorry if I speak out of turn," Gordo said, wiping some sweat from his glistening brow, "but wasn't she—um—*isn't* she married to Count Craven?"

"She is indeed," Susti confirmed, grinning mischievously as the crowd began to mutter among themselves.

"Not Mad Count Craven," shouted a voice from the crowd. "The thrice-dead zombeegol whose haunted city of Wemeru lies deep in the Voodoo Jungles of Rintintetly?"

Susti nodded a confirmation.

Both Gape and Groan remained silent. Gordo bit his lip.

"For the Something Borrowed," the princess went on, "I would simply adore Pagoda's Box."

"Pagoda's Box?" echoed another voice from the gathering gawpers. "But isn't that the legendary treasure chest on Windlass Eyrie, topmost tower among the Finion Finger Mountains?"

Susti smiled. "It is."

"The one that's watched twenty-four hours a day by the harpies of Narrow Death Rise?"

"What is this," Gape shouted at the crowd, "a city full of geography students?"

"They are nevertheless correct," said Susti, peering over the heads of the crowd in an attempt to determine exactly where the voices were coming from.

Gordo was also on the lookout, but it was intensely difficult to put a voice to a groin.

"Finally," the princess twittered, returning her attention to the scroll, "for the Something Blue, I very much desire the jeweled eyes of Torche."

"Torche?" said another voice from the fray. "You mean, the forty-foot dragon that's been terrorizing Fastrush Pass for the best slice of a century?"

"Who's askin'?" bellowed Groan, suddenly aggravated by the constant interruptions.

The crowd shuffled around, but no one came forward.

King Phew was smiling craftily, but his daughter looked extremely doubtful.

"Are you sure you're interested?" she suddenly asked the warriors, her voice ever so slightly tremulous.

"SILENCE!" yelled the king. "THE CHALLENGE HAS ALREADY BEEN ACCEPTED."

There were a number of shocked faces; none more than Princess Susti's, but her father continued: "THE FIRST NOBLE WARRIOR TO RETURN WITH ALL THAT MY DAUGHTER DESIRES WILL BE AWARDED HER HAND IN MARRIAGE."

"But, Father—"

"AND NO MORE WILL BE SAID ABOUT IT. I HAVE SPOKEN."

FOUR

PHLEGM WAS FAMOUS for its gardens, and those surrounding the keep were no exception. Rows of neat hedges stretched away in all directions, with fountains and ornate statues occupying every space large enough to accommodate them. There were several wide stone benches dotted around the borders of the garden, decorated with strange carvings that dated back to the Dual Age. All were vacant except for one, where a heated conversation was taking place.

"All I'm saying," Gordo reasoned, "is that we don't have to travel separately. We could make for Rintintetly—that's nearest—and then decide who goes for the opal. You know, strength in numbers and all that."

Gordo felt as though he were trying to persuade his

audience that dogs could play the banjo. As expected, the journey to the fabled city of common sense was an effort for the Groan psyche, but now even Gape was looking at him with baffled amusement.

"It's only a suggestion," finished the dwarf.

"I've got a suggestion myself," Gape started, grinning to expose a mouthful of gleaming white teeth.

"Oh, yes?" Gordo asked hopefully. "And what's that?"

"I think you should climb to the highest tower in the kingdom and jump out of the window."

The dwarf glared at him.

"I don't reckon' that'd 'elp much," Groan roared, his brows knotted so tight that they appeared to be mating on his forehead.

"No," said Gape, "but it would improve my day, no end."

Gordo sighed. "Well, whether you two muscle heads choose to believe it or not, we're going to need all the help we can get. I mean, the Finion Finger Mountains? Fastrush Pass? Those places are supposed to be damn near impossible to get to! And as for Kazbrack—"

"We bin there," Groan interrupted. "Dint see 'ny fire demons, though, did we?"

"No, Groan, we didn't," admitted Gordo. "Maybe they've moved in since we were there." He turned to Gape and explained: "We were almost drowned at the hands of some bloody lunatic hermit, who thought he could get us back to the mainland in a boat made of shoe soles."

Groan gave an enthusiastic nod. "Was a good laugh," he muttered.

"Anyway," Gordo continued, ignoring him, "Kazbrack is out past Rintintetly, just off the coast. At least we can kill two birds with one stone." He turned to Gape. "I'm warning you, though: Kazbrack's no pushover."

Gape looked the dwarf up and down. "High wall, is there?"

"Funny."

"Maybe we can give you a leg up, or even—wait a moment—I think I might have a catapult in my belt pouch!"

"Why don't you shut the hell up, Gape Teethgrit!" Gordo snapped. "If you're so clever, how come we found you in Stoke Punnit tied to a tree with two twigs up your nose?"

The barbarian shrugged. "I told you, I was ambushed."

Gordo nodded. "By a ten-year-old girl."

"There was more than one of them. . . ."

"Oh, I see. How many, then? Two? Three?"

Gape shook his head. "More like ten, actually. They all had uniforms."

"Oh, the Ganiskin Girl Guides! Yeah, I've heard of them; deadly with a headband, they are."

"That's it!" Gape leaped to his feet and snatched up his swords. "I don't have to listen to any of this rubbish; I'm a world-renowned mercenary!"

"No," Gordo said, dangling his legs over the bench. "You're a mediocre warrior who's lucky enough to own two enchanted swords that never miss."

"Yeah," Groan echoed, but his little companion quickly turned on him.

"And you can't talk, Groan Teethgrit. You've got the IQ of a bacon sandwich; I've seen *plants* that think faster than you."

"Oh, yeah?" the barbarian exclaimed. "What *ones*?"

Gordo sighed deeply and held up his hands for calm. "Listen," he said. "The fact I'm trying to get through to you both is that we'll be so much stronger if we all pull together."

Gape sheathed his swords. He still didn't look convinced, but at least, Gordo reflected, he wasn't leaving.

"Only one of us can take them treasures," Groan muttered. "The princess can't marry four o' us."

"Agreed." Gordo nodded, wondering who the other two were. "But until we *find* each treasure, surely it's best if we form a team. You know, a fighting unit."

There was a moment of contemplation. That is, Gape stood in silent agreement while Groan contemplated. Gordo fancied that he could actually hear the heavy gears of the barbarian's mind turning.

"All right wiv me," he said eventually. "Long as I get firs' watch when we camp."

"I'll go second!" Gordo cut in quickly.

"Fine," said Gape, extending his chiseled jaw. "I can't sleep after four anyway. Where are we going first?"

Gordo swung himself off the seat and snatched up his battle-axe. "Rintintetly," he confirmed with a grin. "As I said before, it's the nearest. I'm going to the library to find some info on the place, then we can get going. You two better wait here. Okay?"

There was a vague murmur of agreement as the

dwarf gave a satisfied nod and waddled off toward the keep.

Gape waited until the dwarf had disappeared inside the building before he turned to Groan, and with a slight wave of his hand, indicated the barbarian's sword.

"Good blade, brother," he observed.

"Yeah, 'tis," Groan agreed.

"What d'you think of mine?" Gape drew both weapons in one smooth motion and spun them in a symmetrical arc.

"Rubbish," said Groan.

Gape swallowed, counted to ten under his breath, and then exhaled. "Is that a fact?"

"Yeah, 'sright."

"Well, let me tell you something, Mr. I've Got A Big Broadsword That's About As Sharp As My Intellect, neither of these two beauties ever miss."

"Ha! My armpit."

Gape grinned. "Think what you will, dense brother of mine. It's like your midget says: they're enchanted."

"'Sluck."

"It's not luck, Groan. We went through all this as kids, remember? They're enchanted. I found them in the base of a magic oak tree, and they were glowing with supernatural force. Uncle Nap said they were enchanted, the chief said they were enchanted, even Dad said they were enchanted—and he didn't believe in sorcery! So you're just going to have to accept it, aren't you? I have a pair of magic swords, and you don't."

"'Sluck."

"They're enchanted, damn you!"

Groan shook his head. "'Sluck."

"Okay, fine," Gape muttered. "Have it your way."

There was a moment of silence, in which Groan smiled inwardly and Gape felt that every muscle in his body was about to burst.

"'S jus' luck," Groan muttered again, pushing the argument to the breaking point.

"Fine," Gape said. "But if it's luck, dear brother, then how come neither of these beauties has missed a single target in twenty years?"

"Prove it," Groan sniffed, squinting in the sunlight that flooded the gardens. "I bet you couldn' 'it that ol' woman over there what's hangin' out 'er washin'."

There was no thinking involved, not even the

slightest moment of doubt. Gape simply spun on his heels and launched both swords into the air.

When Gordo Goldeaxe emerged from the Phlegm Keep library, he had a very bad feeling in his stomach. There were two reasons for this: the first had to do with the hideously frightening information he'd discovered while researching Rintintetly; the second, which was definitely more pressing, involved the vast crowd that had gathered in the square, seemingly around Groan Teethgrit and his insufferable brother. Gordo had known Groan for ten years, ample time to learn that people tended to veer *away* from the giant barbarian at all costs, and never, under any circumstances, gathered around him . . . unless something really bad (and thus extremely watchable) had happened.

Gordo determinedly elbowed his way through the crowd, and almost fell over the elderly woman who lay on the cobbles with two very familiar-looking swords sticking out of her chest.

"An absolute bloody animal!" one man was saying.

"An outrage!" added another. "He just murdered her for no reason."

Gape Teethgrit was on his knees beside the old woman, sobbing his heart out. Behind him, several of the more gutsy members of the crowd were arming themselves with clubs and maces. They were deterred from venturing farther, however, by the towering figure of Groan, who was standing, arms folded, behind his brother.

"You're right 'bout them swords," he was saying to Gape's convulsing shoulders. "How much d'you want for 'em?"

"Oh my gods," Gape cried, hands cupped over his face. "What have I done?"

"They boaf 'it 'er at the same time," Groan observed. "Tha's good workmanship, that is. I wond'r who made 'em?"

"Oh, may the heavens forgive m—"

"Excuse me, please, I'm a healer."

The stirring crowd parted to reveal a dwarf in a priest's robe. Groan recognized his friend straight away, but there were a lot of dwarves in Phlegm, and those in the crowd were not familiar enough with Gordo to recognize his waddle.

A hushed silence descended on the crowd as Gordo shoved Gape aside and bent down to examine the corpse. He spent a few seconds removing the enchanted blades, then appeared to study the two wounds in greater detail. Eventually, he turned to the crowd.

"I'm afraid this woman is suffering from something we healers call Attracticus Enchantia," he began, to an applause of gasps. "Meaning that, through no fault of her own, she is prone to attract enchanted swords."

There ensued some huddled conversation, and a crowd spokesman was nudged forward.

"I've never heard of it," he said doubtfully.

Several of his coconspirators muttered an agreement.

"Ah, well, it's quite rare," Gordo continued, trying to keep the hood, which was three sizes too big for his head, in place. "It's a form of animal magnetism, you see. . . ."

The crowd spokesman cocked his head to one side and regarded the woman. "Well, it's not workin' on me," he said.

There was an outbreak of giggles, during which Groan ambled over to Gordo and tapped him on the head. "'Ere, where d'you get that 'ood from?"

"Shhhh! Keep quiet; can't you see I'm working,

here? CAN SOMEBODY PLEASE SEND FOR A MORTUARIST?"

The crowd pushed and shoved each other for a bit, then disgorged a small boy to fetch the local corpse cart.

"Very good," Gordo shouted, giving them a "thumbs-up" sign. "Now, can this lady please have some privacy?"

Slowly but surely, the crowd began to ebb away, and, at length, the mortuarist arrived to collect the body.

"Excuse me," Gape said to the man, still shaking with grief. "Do you know who this woman is, er, was?"

The mortuarist took a long, careful look at the woman. "It's Reeny Shand," he confirmed, chewing on his cheeks. "Wicked ol' girl, she was. Just got outta the dungeon for turnin' a load of kids to stone. Finally got her comeuppance, did she?"

"Y-yes, I suppose so," Gape sniffled. "Does she have any family?"

The mortuarist shook his head. "No husband, no kids, but there's a cat who won't be best pleased."

"Oh. Right. Thanks."

Gape, Groan, and Gordo watched as Reeny was loaded into the cart and wheeled away.

"What a terrible tragedy," Gape mumbled, looking at his hands as if they didn't belong to him.

"You're right 'bout that," chimed Groan. "*I* shoulda found them swords."

Gape reached down and carefully picked up his blades. "Er . . . thanks, Gordo," he said awkwardly.

"Yeah, well . . . whatever," said the dwarf, and snatching back his hood, he called after the mortuarist: "Oi, there's a priest down that side alley you might wanna take a look at!"

When he turned back, two pairs of eyes were locked on him.

"What? I had to get the hood from somewhere, didn't I? And while I've got your attention, may I remind you both that we are supposed to be on a vital quest to win the hand of a princess? Now, do forgive me if I'm wrong, but I can't see how using an old lady for target practice is gonna help our cause. So let's forget about whether I may or may not have killed a priest, and let's get on with the mission!"

There was a general murmur of agreement, but Gordo couldn't help but look wretched. He peered back toward the alley, and was about to make another excuse for his own attack on the rector, when a jangling noise shook him from his reverie.

"Um, excuse me—"

Groan turned, frowned. "'Scuse you what?" he demanded gruffly.

A knight in purple pantaloons, with coiffured blond hair and large, hooped earrings had strolled into the small triangle of ground between the three warriors.

Gape had been about to tell the stranger to get lost, when he'd noticed, to his intense astonishment, that the man was filing his nails.

"Can we help you with something, Mr.—?" Gordo hazarded, leaning on his battle-axe with an "I'm-gonna-take-no-nonsense" expression on his face.

"Sir Herbert Lavelle DuBree, at your service. I was in the courtyard earlier today, and I heard about your—hem—most noble quest."

Gordo rolled his eyes. "Right, well listen, Sherbert—"

"HERBERT."

"*Whatever*. We're not interested—"

"—in an enchanted treasure map? What, really? Oh, okay; that's fine, then. Forget I ever offered to sell you one. Good day, people."

The knight turned, his heels clicking together as

he sauntered away. He managed to get about three yards before Gape dragged him back.

"Enchanted, you say?" Gordo prompted, licking his lips and glancing significantly at Groan.

"I *do* say, and enchanted it *is*. Shows you the location of every treasure ever buried by mortal hands."

"How much d'you want for it?"

Herbert sniffed a few times, then gave the most pathetic sneeze Gordo had ever heard. It sounded like a mouse squeaking.

"Twenty crowns to you fine gentlemen," he said. "And please don't bother to haggle—I'm not known for my flexibility."

"You sure?" said Gape, eyeing him dubiously.

The knight ignored the comment and held out his hand expectantly.

"What?" Gordo said, starting. "You expect us to cough up twenty crowns, just like that?"

There was a premature silence, then Gordo produced a pouch from his belt and slammed it so viciously into Herbert's outstretched hands that the knight gave a tiny whimper.

"Bloody mercenaries," he muttered under his breath, pulling a scroll from his pantaloons and passing it across to the dwarf. "Don't recognize a good deal when it hops up and bites their *argghghhh*!"

Gordo, who'd grabbed the knight's wrist instead of the map, pulled the man's face close to him.

"If this thing doesn't work," he snarled. "We'll find you."

He shoved Herbert back onto the dusty ground and waited while the knight crawled away on his knuckles. Then he turned to the brothers Teethgrit and smirked. "Result!" he mouthed. "We got ourselves a magic treasure map!"

FIVE

"I'M TELLING you straight, Bronwyn, I'm not marrying either of those cretins, and that's all there is to it. I don't care what my father says."

Princess Susti slammed the heavy oak door of her private chamber, then tore off her ceremonial headdress and threw it across the room.

Her lady-in-waiting ducked. "Then why did you set the challenge, milady?"

"I didn't! Father came to my chamber this morning, said it was time I got married, and fed me some rubbish about the fate of the kingdom being in great peril if I didn't oblige! The old fool was practically in tears, Bronwyn. What could I say?"

"I'm sure you did what you had to do, milady."

"Right, exactly! And did you listen to that awful speech he made me reel off? All that rot about 'when

I was young. . . .' Ha! When *I* was young, *I* used to pull the legs off spiders! Let him stick that in his speech!"

She unclasped her headband and let out her long, silky brown locks. "You know why he's doing this, don't you?"

"No, milady."

"He's doing it because he's had some sort of bet with Duke Modeset and all those other half-wits."

"That would explain why they're here, Highness."

Susti paused, studying her servant's expression with care. "That would explain why *who* is here?" she inquired.

"Duke Modeset, Highness. He's staying in the East Tower with his manservant."

"Hmm . . . I wonder why he didn't make his presence known at the arena."

"Maybe he didn't want to be seen, Highness."

"Ha! I knew it. There's something going on. I'll bet my father's told them all that he can get me married off before the Spring Games. Don't laugh, Bronwyn. I'm serious!"

"Surely not, milady," said the servant, emerging from the shadows. She shared the princess's hour-glass figure, but her skin was so pale that she was almost ghostly in appearance. "If that were the case, then surely your father would marry you off to a local noble?"

Susti shook her head. "You don't know my father, Bronwyn, you really don't. He has a kind heart, but he's very weak willed when it comes to the other lords, Modeset especially."

"And you, milady? What about you?"

"Oh, I don't have any feelings, Bronwyn; I'm just bait. Well, we'll soon see about that, won't we?"

"Milady?"

Susti gave the girl one of her golden smiles. "We're going on a little trip," she said.

"We?"

"Yes, you and I."

"Oh, but won't your father—"

"Do not mention his name in my presence, Bronwyn!" Susti snapped. "From now on, as far as I'm concerned, I'm an orphan."

"B-but, milady." Bronwyn hurried over to the princess, who had jumped to her feet and was determinedly pacing the room. "W-what are you going to do?"

Susti stopped pacing and took a deep, meditative breath. "It's quite simple, Bronwyn," she said. "I'm going to escape!"

It was unfashionably early in Phlegm when the Teethgrit party left for the first leg of their journey, and there wasn't a soul on the streets. Even the main gate, which was usually packed with guards, sported no more than a few snoozing sentries and a rather mangy-looking hound.

Gordo led the group, partly because he'd determined the route they were taking, but mostly because Groan and Gape couldn't stop arguing about which one of them should go in front. Gordo strongly suspected that the argument would not be an isolated incident. At least, he reflected, they had a decent map.

In fact, the knight's enchanted scroll showed the entire continent of Illmoor and several surrounding islands. Dotted all over these (some clustered in groups and some more evenly spaced) were many tiny pinpricks of light, presumably depicting the sites of buried treasure. Gordo squinted as he struggled to find the island of Kazbrack. His squint quickly changed to a scowl, when, having located the little landmass just off the east coast, he discovered that the area was completely devoid of a dot.

"What's the problem?" Gape asked, but Gordo's mind was definitely elsewhere. In fact, it had strolled through peevishness, cantered through annoyance, and was now galloping toward fury.

"Bloody liar," he spat.

"Eh?" said Groan and Gape in unison.

"There's no treasure mark!" the dwarf snapped. "Not one!"

"How d'you mean?" said Gape, hurrying forward and peering over Gordo's shoulder.

"Dots mean treasure, and there're dots all over the place, so there should be a dot! There's no bloody dot, damn it!"

The brothers were looking at the dwarf as if he'd just suggested they all buy an ostrich.

"Not a single ONE!" Gordo shouted incredulously. "Not on Kazbrack, Rintintetly, Windlass Eyrie *or* bloody Fastrush Pass! This map's useless. I *told* you that knight was dodgy!"

"No, you didn't," Gape said resentfully. "You merely told the knight that if it *didn't* work, we would find him. Besides, you didn't seriously think—"

"I'm going back. Herbert of Bree, wasn't it?"

Gordo spun around and began to march determinedly back toward Phlegm, but Groan stuck out a leg and tripped him up.

"Oi, I aint goin' back ta Phlegm," he growled.

Gordo spat out some dirt and forced himself up onto his feet. Both warriors were grimacing at him.

"All right," he said eventually. "But if I ever see that knight again, he's dead meat."

"Yeah, right. We'll get 'im one day."

"Fair enough."

Gordo didn't talk for the next hour. Instead, he stamped on ahead of them, studying the map as he went and trying to block the infuriating pinpricks out of his mind. At least, he reflected, the map seemed *accurate*.

As he plodded along, his mind raced back to the few obscure facts about their destination he'd managed to learn from the library in Phlegm.

It didn't bode well.

Rintintetly, their first port of call, was by far the thickest and most feared jungle on Illmoor. The city of Wemeru, nestled like a forgotten jewel at its heart, laying claim to several ancient races and a government rumored to be knee-deep in necromancy.

Wemeru was ruled by the occasionally reclusive Count Craven, who, it was said, sustained his prolonged existence by bathing in the blood of chickens. The citizens of Wemeru had no idea why this worked, but since the Count was more than six hundred years old, nobody was asking any questions. As a result of all this, Wemeru was famous for its pale inhabitants and its cold streets packed with zombie fowl.

Gordo wasn't looking forward to the journey.

"Which way we goin' again?" Groan asked, peering around him with the same blank expression he always had first thing in the morning, when he couldn't remember who he was.

"See those foothills?" said Gordo, pointing eastward.

"Yeah, course."

"Well, we're going over those to the western bank of the Washin."

Groan muttered something under his breath, and moved off again. As Gordo watched his friend, he noticed for the first time that Groan was actually a good deal broader than his brother, whose flowing locks occasionally made him look slightly brawnier than he was.

"Hold on a minute," said Gape, stopping suddenly while the others walked on. "Hey! Wait! Come back here for a second!"

Gordo shuffled to a halt, though he had to snatch the back of Groan's loincloth to get his friend to stop.

"What's wrong?" the dwarf inquired, his half grin slightly faded by the rigorous effects of the scorching sun. "Swords too heavy for you, are they?"

Gape pointed off toward a curl of smoke in the distance. "There's a coaching inn."

Gordo shrugged. "So?"

"So, maybe we can get a lift. I mean, why walk if there's wheels to take you?"

"Look," the dwarf began, ignoring the fact that Groan had already started walking in the direction his brother had indicated. "What do we want a coach for? We're warriors, aren't we? Besides, it'll cost MONEY! Come back here, damn it!"

Gordo sighed, and drove his axe into the hillside. "I don't know why I bother," he grumbled.

"At least there's no one around," Susti whispered, leading her former lady-in-waiting and newly appointed sword-maiden through the dusty corridors of Phlegm Keep.

"Isn't that a bit odd, milady?" asked Bronwyn doubtfully. "I mean, it *is* two o'clock in the afternoon."

The princess shrugged. "Probably just one of my father's all-day drinking sessions," she said. "You know what the court's like once he gets going; they'll be singing songs about naked women, playing the banjo, and leering 'till the cows come home. I think it's utterly disgusting, don't you?"

"Oh, absolutely, milady," said Bronwyn, who'd danced privately for the king. "It's not even as if they're grateful."

"You said it. Still, all the better for our escape! C'mon, let's move."

They hurried through the silent halls, rounded a sharp bend, and crept into the kitchen. Then Susti stopped dead.

"What is it, milady?" Bronwyn whispered.

"There's nobody here."

"Sorry?"

"The kitchen, it's empty. Now, *that* is unusual. In fact, I'm beginning to smell a rat, here."

"Oh, no, milady! I can't stand vermin."

"I was speaking figuratively, Bronwyn."

"Of course, milady. Sorry."

Susti inched her way into the kitchen, then dropped down onto her hands and knees and began to advance, catlike, across the kitchen floor. She'd got roughly halfway through the room, when a voice shouted "Now!" and a vast net dropped over her. As she struggled to free herself, the princess became more entangled, and increasingly annoyed.

Bronwyn hurried over to help her mistress, but was deterred from doing so by the sight of King Phew and several of his bodyguards entering from the opposite end of the kitchen.

"Father!" raged Susti, clawing ineffectually at her gauzy prison. "What is the meaning of this?"

There was no reply, but two of the king's guards rushed forward, pulled the princess out of the net, and helped her to her feet. She made considerable effort to elbow each of them in the chest as they released her.

"I demand an explanation, Father," she snapped. "Why did you do that?"

"You tried to escape," King Phew said simply. "And I cannot allow that to happen." He marched over to the nearest bench and used it as a stepping-stone to clamber onto the tabletop, where he took his rest.

"I'm sorry, my darling, but I had to demonstrate that I won't be disobeyed on this matter, and I knew that if I told you not to run away, you'd inevitably try."

"B-but I don't want to marry any of those people. I made that speech because you begged me to, and I don't like to see you upset, but if you think I'm marrying some idiot barb—"

"You won't have to, precious. I'm sorry; I should have explained. . . ."

"Explained *what*, father?" Susti hesitated, a frown briefly creasing her elfin features. "What is this all about?"

"Leave us," King Phew instructed the guards, adding, "and you!" when his daughter's assistant made to take a seat herself.

"Sit down, darling," he said, when the room had cleared.

"I don't want to."

"Please."

Susti sighed, and slumped onto the nearest bench. "Well?"

"It's a trap." The king smiled, but he was notably nervous.

"A trap? For who?"

"Groan Teethgrit. He's—um—he's an abomination and a—um—a menace to society; him and those other . . . miscreants."

Susti hugged her arms for warmth; the air in the kitchen was unusually cold.

"Those don't sound like your words, Father."

"Mmm? Oh, well, that is, they're not, as such, but Duke Modeset is here, on behalf of the other rulers, and he says—"

The princess shook her head sadly. "So you're being told what to do by those squabbling nobles?"

"We've spoken about this before, Susti. Phlegm is a respected member of the Great Assembly, and I have a responsibility—"

"Yes, you do: to your people, your kingdom, and, I hope, to your daughter. Does Groan Teethgrit pose a direct threat to this city?"

"Y-yes. I believe he does."

"He was perfectly nice to me. In fact, they both were. I mean, even Groan's little dwarf gave me a flower! What's going to happen to them all?"

"Um, they're, er—"

"Those tasks are impossible, aren't they?"

The king didn't look at his daughter, but nodded.

"So you sent them to their deaths?"

"Well, not me personally, but—"

"And you used me as bait!" Susti leaped from the bench, her eyes welling up with tears. "I can't believe you'd think so little of me!"

"I didn't have a choice," the king pleaded, snatching at his daughter's arm. "They're the Great Assembly. They told me not to clue you in on what was going on, but I had to at least do that."

"Ha! We're the richest kingdom in Illmoor."

"Yes, we are!" Phew agreed. "But only because *they* allow it."

"Don't be ridiculous, Father."

"I'm not being ridiculous; I'm being perfectly serious. Individually, we could probably handle any one of them, but together they'd easily be able to wipe us out. Besides, in a way I actually agree with them; this Teethgrit fellow and his kin have done some appalling things. You should hear what he did to—"

"The children of Dullitch? Yes, he and the dwarf brought them all home, didn't they?"

"That's not the point, my darling. The point *is*, they've become a menace."

"I see," said Susti, who didn't. "So what *is* the plan, then?"

King Phew licked his lips. "Well," he said, "basically, we just wait. The locations were chosen because they're the four most dangerous places on Illmoor, places from which men seldom return."

Susti raised an eyebrow. "So they do exist, then?"

"Well, the places do," King Phew sighed. "Though it goes without saying that most of the treasures are fake."

Susti's eyes widened. "Not *all* of them?" she said hopefully.

The king shrugged. "Well, I'm sure I heard something about an Idol of Needs being found once—"

"You *heard* something? I can't believe this!" Susti gasped. "But, but what about the people in the crowd, the people that knew of them?"

"Plants, I'm afraid: put in the crowd to assist our cause. Duke Modeset's idea."

"But I gave them those missions! You told me—"

"Yes, my dear, though you needn't worry. You're entirely blameless."

The princess was beside herself. "So the duke's plan is merely to send the Teethgrits into the jaws of death . . . and he's chosen four different places, to make sure they don't come back?"

The king nodded. "Modeset says that if the wilds of Kazbrack or the Rintintetly zombies don't kill them, then the harpies or the dragon will. There's nothing we can do for them now, my darling. Either way, it's over. . . ."

SIX

IN ITS FIFTY-YEAR history, the Welcroft Coaching Inn had played host to many strange and unusual creatures. Situated, as it was, on the outskirts of Phlegm, it had also received many unwelcome visitors, but none so immediately offensive as the man who currently stood in the saloon bar, a man whose second visit to the inn was proving as catastrophic as his previous one.

Loogie Lambontroff shook out the flaps of his thick overcoat, cracked his knuckles, and sighed. "I'm not a violent man, Mr. Jenkins."

"Yes you are!" the innkeeper exclaimed, helping his wife to her feet. "You've broken her arm!"

Loogie shook his head. "Oh, come on," he argued, eyeing the crossbow he'd balanced precariously on a stool beside the table. "Your *wife* attacked me with a foreign object. . . ."

"Don't be ridiculous! All she did was answer the door!"

"—with a frying pan in her hand?"

"We were getting breakfast!"

"Yeah, well, how was I to know that? I'm not taking any chances, am I? Now, as I was saying before you took it upon yourself to interrupt, I am not a violent man. At least, not anymore. . . ."

The innkeeper indicated a wreckage of wood and bronze that lay just inside the entrance. "You've ripped our front door off its hinges!"

"Yes, yes I did! And, as a matter of fact, I'm very glad you mentioned it," Loogie said, managing to smile and frown at the same time, "because *that* has to be the weakest excuse for a door in the entire history of woodwork. The frame was shoddy, the mailbox came away in my hand, and I got a mouthful of abuse off the knocker before I'd come three feet up the drive. Who built this place, anyway? Three pigs?"

"Our barmaid had to take a week off after your last visit—she said you head-butted three of the regulars, broke a window, and left something terrible in the easement."

"I see. Anything else?"

The innkeeper pointed a shaking finger at the gangster. "You're an animal, *Lord* Lambontroff. One of our regulars used to be a woodsman on the edge of the Washin: he told us ALL about you."

Loogie made a dismissive gesture with both hands, then suddenly leaped onto the table and sat down, cross-legged, drawing in a deep breath as if to prevent himself any further loss of temper. "That's neither here nor there," he snapped, as the couple looked on, wide-eyed. "I've not come to your decrepit dung heap of an inn to discuss my past—and, incidentally, you can forget anything you've heard from your *scummy* regulars: I haven't been *Lord* Lambontroff for a long time." He flexed his knuckles. "I work for Mr. Mediocre now, and I'm here—once again—to discuss your little *debt* problem. I thought I'd arrive unannounced this time, as you were both conveniently *absent* during my last visit. I had to leave a message with your stupid barmaid, and Mr. Mediocre *hates* it when I have to leave messages." He finished the statement with a feline grin.

"Mr. Mediocre?" repeated the innkeeper, his wife cowering in the shadows behind him. "Who—"

"He's Mr. Big's assistant . . . and I don't know

what you're grinning at, because Mr. Mediocre can get very nasty when he wants to."

The innkeeper's tone changed immediately. "Of course, sir. I wasn't grinning, honestly; it's my bone structure."

Loogie nodded. "So get on with it, then . . . I want that safe emptied, and don't even think about making any excuses."

The innkeeper didn't move, but he did begin to sweat. "Um, well, actually, business has been a bit slow this month, and we—"

Loogie picked up his crossbow and took aim. "That sounds like an excuse to me. . . ."

The innkeeper held up a shaking hand. "P-please! We d-detailed our situation in a l-letter," he stammered. "They sent one back; said it'd be all right to pay double next month."

Loogie paused, lowering the weapon slightly. "I might be new to this job," he muttered, "but I didn't come down in the last shower. Mr. Big's been on holiday in Spittle since June, and I reckon Mr. Mediocre would've told me if he'd decided to let you off a payment. So who sent you this letter?"

The innkeeper thought for a moment, his brown eyes glistening with the effort.

"Mr. Titch," he said, wringing his hands.

"Mr. Titch is dyslexic," Loogie sniggered. "You're lying through your teeth." He raised the crossbow again.

"I know, I know," The innkeeper gasped hurriedly. "But he only dictated the letter. Mr. indrfnff wrote it down."

Loogie boggled at him. "Mr. who?"

"Mr. indrfnff."

"Mr. Indifferent?"

"Yes! That's it! Definitely. Mr. Indifferent."

Loogie's beady eyes narrowed. "And that's your final answer?"

The innkeeper nodded, trying desperately to ignore his wife's whimpering.

"There's not a doubt in your mind?"

"No, sir."

"You're *that* sure?"

"I'm sure, sir!"

Loogie cocked his head to one side. Then he raised the crossbow, drew back the bolt, and aimed.

"Bad luck, then, because there's no such person as Mr. Indifferent, and you just signed your own death warrant."

"Noooo!"

The innkeeper dropped to his knees and began to beg for mercy, his wife echoing his every word.

"P-p-please spare us!"

Loogie shook his head. "I don't do mercy."

"But you said you weren't a violent man!"

"I lied. Now get up and take what's coming to y—"

Two giant shadows fell across the floor of the inn, creating a sudden absence of light, which, in effect, cut off Loogie's words.

Gordo Goldeaxe squeezed between Groan's and Gape's tree-trunk legs and waddled through the devastated doorway.

"Sorry to interrupt your little party," he began, staring distractedly around the inn. "But we need to take the next available coach. What time does it leave?"

Loogie gritted his teeth and, briefly taking his hand off the crossbow support, waved them both away.

"Scram," he said simply. "Can't you see they're not open for business?"

Gordo appeared to notice the innkeeper and his wife for the first time. "What's going on—" he began, but Loogie interrupted.

"Get lost, short-arse, or you and your boy-friends are next."

It was very nearly the last thing Loogie Lambontroff ever said.

"It's wrong, Bronwyn," Susti whispered, opening the door to her bedchamber and peering into the room to make certain that no one was lurking there. "I mean, not that long ago we were at war with Dullitch, and now my father's taking orders from them!"

"But, milady, you said—"

"Yes, yes, I know it's not just them . . . but Duke Modeset's in charge of the Assembly, and he was on the throne when their soldiers attacked our merchant caravans!"

"Of course, milady, but you know what they say—"

"Mmm? What?"

"Well, you know—forgive and forget. Perhaps your father just wants peace. . . ."

"And I'm fine with that, Bronwyn, but I don't see why we should bow down to the likes of Dullitch and Spittle merely because *they're* having problems with Groan Teethgrit. I say we should let them sort it out themselves!"

Bronwyn gave a meek nod of agreement. "I'm sure you're right, milady."

"I mean, how dare they order us around!" Susti blazed on. "I was a little girl when Dullitch laid siege to the keep, and I remember the whole episode very well. Do you know who came to our rescue? Not Spittle, that's for sure . . . and I don't recall a great deal of help from Sneeze or Legrash, either. On the contrary: it was mercenaries who came to our rescue, a big tribe from the Mountains of Mavokhan."

"I remember, milady. One of the female barbarians gave me an ornamental dagger; they were very kind."

Susti nodded. "You see what I mean? It's crazy. I've a good mind to warn them."

"Oh, no, milady," Bronwyn protested. "You mustn't do that!"

The princess reflected for a moment, then shook her head.

"No, no, you're absolutely right, Bronwyn. If I warned them, my father would get the blame for everything. The Assembly would probably throw him out."

"Exactly, Majesty."

"In fact, I've got a much better idea."

"Milady?"

Bronwyn studied her mistress's suddenly possessed expression, and began to feel quite faint.

"Well, I could help them!"

"Yes, milady, but—"

"Quiet, Bronwyn! It's a great idea; I've studied geography all of my life—I could tell them the best routes to follow!" Susti clapped her hands together and raced over to a heavy, claw-legged chest, which stood against the east wall. After fumbling frantically with the ornate clasp, she threw open the lid of the chest and began to drag out various items. "We'll need some rope, a tinderbox, swords, a grappling iron, a lantern, a road map, and some money. Hmm . . . and we need to write a farewell note to Father."

Bronwyn folded her arms carefully. "We, Majesty?"

"Oh, don't start all that again, Bron. I'm a bloody princess—I'm hardly likely to go hiking all over Illmoor on my own, am I?"

Everything happened in a blur.

Gordo was the first to move, hurling his battle-axe at Loogie Lambontroff before the gangster had a chance to turn and fire his crossbow. Missing by a gnat's wing, the axe smashed into the bar behind Loogie, taking out a month's supply of spirits in the process. Gape had drawn both swords, but his brother was in the way.

Lambontroff, who'd ducked down to avoid the spinning weapon, reacted quickly, firing off a bolt from his bow and watching, in frank astonishment, as Groan snatched it out of the air and crushed it into splinters.

In the frenetic excitement that followed, the innkeeper took initiative, snatched up his wife's frying pan, and belted Loogie across the back of the head, grinning with relief as the gangster collapsed.

"Thanks for that, fellas," he breathed, helping his wife to her feet. "We're proper grateful."

"A pleasure," Gordo muttered, crunching over the remains of the inn's door frame. "Nasty piece of work, by the looks of it. Er . . . about that coach?"

The innkeeper sighed despondently. "I'm afraid they're not running at the moment," he said. "Business has been pretty dead recently, and most of the trade routes are closed."

Gape let out a long sigh, and wandered outside for some fresh air.

Gordo cracked his knuckles. "A pity," he said. "We really do need to get to Sneeze."

The innkeeper gave a sympathetic shrug, but his wife had a thoughtful look on her face.

"There's always Barnaby's old coach," she said.

"Nah," muttered the innkeeper. "Nobody in their right mind would try riding that on the steeps." He looked Groan up and down, then added: "Mind you . . . it does go some, when it's not rattling to pieces."

"Sounds perfect," said Gordo quickly. "How much d'you want for it?"

The innkeeper pursed his lips and whistled. "Now you're asking me. Er . . . fifty crowns?"

"Does it come with a horse?" Gordo asked, irritably scratching an eyebrow.

"Does it heck as like! For fifty crowns, you'd be lucky if it comes with wheels!"

"Yeah," Groan thundered, indicating Loogie. "An' you're lucky we came in 'ere when we did, 'siderin' that bloke was ready to reckon' you up."

"Twenty crowns," the innkeeper's wife said decisively, "and forty for the horse."

"You what?" Gordo exclaimed. "That's sixty! You only wanted fifty in the first place!"

"That was without the horse," the innkeeper protested. "He's a good horse, is old Barnaby: a champion in his day."

"Is sixty more 'an fifty?" said Groan, who was getting confused.

"Of course it is!" Gordo snapped, and turning back to the innkeeper's wife, added, "Forty-five for the both, and that's my final offer."

"Fifty, and I'll throw in some luggage ropes for the side hooks."

Gordo looked amazed. "You mean it hasn't even got a roof rack?" he exclaimed.

The innkeeper's wife rolled her eyes. "Of course it doesn't have a roof rack," she said. "It hasn't got a roof!"

"Ha! Then it's not a coach, is it? It's a bloody cart; and in that case, I'll have it for thirty-five and not a single penny more."

"Forty-five."

"Done."

Gordo extended his hand, but the innkeeper pulled back his wife's arm and whispered anxiously into her ear. There followed a brief (and largely wordless) argument, after which the innkeeper's wife turned back to the mercenaries and announced, "You can have the coach *and* the horse *and* the luggage ropes for twenty crowns, if you agree to take him with you."

Groan glanced down at Loogie and shrugged, but Gordo looked none to happy about the proposal.

"Who is he?" he asked, eyeing the innkeeper carefully.

The innkeeper pursed his lips, then motioned for Gordo to step to one side.

"His name's Loogie Lambontroff, and he's the nephew of a noble," he whispered, crouching to bring his mouth level with Gordo's ear. "But he ran away from home three years ago, after his uncle stole his pet chicken; made big news in these parts. The family put a huge bounty on his head—wanted him back at all costs—but nobody would go near him."

"Why not?"

"Maybe it's because nobody wants to take him back to where he came from. Who knows? All I know is what I hear, and I hear he was very well educated in Dullitch before he went to the bad. Nowadays, he works for a bunch of local gangsters who . . ."

The innkeeper proceeded to tell of his own troubles, but Gordo wasn't really listening.

"I've never heard of a noble called Lambon-troff," he said suddenly, cutting the man off. "Where's he from?"

The innkeeper shuddered. "A city called Wemeru, in the jungles of Rintintetly: a terrible place by all accounts, and Lambontroff isn't actually the family name. . . ."

"Hang about," Gordo muttered, taking a step back and regarding the prone man. "His uncle wouldn't be Mad Count Craven, would it?"

SEVEN

BRONWYN GULPED, trying desperately not to look down as she descended the outer wall of Phlegm Keep on a rope fashioned from knotted bedsheets.

"Are you sure about this, ma'am?" she called up at Susti, who was leaning from the arched window of her bedchamber, while at the same time wrestling with the end of the makeshift rope in a valiant attempt to get it hooked up to a wall brazier.

"Hold on, Bronny; I'm almost there!"

The line juddered, and Bronwyn's stomach felt as if it were going to leap into her throat. Then Susti climbed out of the window and began to lower herself down.

"Hurry up, Bronny! I don't want to land on top of you."

"No, ma'am. Of course, ma'am."

Bronwyn took a second gulp of air and managed to summon enough courage to slide another few feet.

"That's my girl! Keep going!"

"Right, ma'am."

"When we get down from here, we're going to get some horses, and then—"

"Aaaaahh!"

"Bronny?"

"Ahhhhhhhhhh!"

"Bronny! Are you okay?"

There was a strangled half scream from a (conveniently placed) haystack at the foot of the keep.

Susti swung round on her section of the line, almost tipping herself upside down.

"Are you alive, Bronny?" she called. "Say something!"

"Mmmfffff."

"Aha! The gods must be with us! Did you land in the haystack?"

"Mmmffff."

"Anything broken?"

"Mmmffff."

"Excellent! I'll be down in a jiffy. . . ."

Far below, the side of the haystack exploded, and Bronwyn came out fighting. Thanks to the prevailing wind, Susti couldn't hear the servant's stream of expletives, and she only just missed the swift and sneaky hand gesture that followed.

"Don't bother waving, Bronny!" the princess yelled. "Just grab the backpacks and find a stable; I'll follow you!"

When Susti eventually reached the ground, her servant was a vague shape, albeit a wobbling one, in the distance. She smiled at the retreating figure, then turned her attention back to the matter at hand.

Fact: she'd managed to get to ground level. Fact: she'd never get out of the city unless she could create some sort of temporary diversion. Fact: the guards were all extremely wimpy and insufferably stupid.

Susti drew in a deep breath and thought for a moment. Then she lit a match and set fire to the bedsheet rope, crouched behind a nearby barrel, and waited. Sure enough, within fifteen minutes, every guard in the keep was either fussing madly over the flames or making every effort to remain invisible until the crisis was over.

Seizing her opportunity, Susti made a mad, frantic dash for the main gate. When she arrived there, Bronwyn had already managed to purchase two fine-looking horses and a not-so-fine-looking horseman called Ned. Susti disposed of Ned with the textbook "look over there—a badger with a broadsword" and a swift chop across the back of the neck.

The duty guard, a weaselly-looking fellow in an oversized chain mail coat, bowed low when he saw the princess approaching.

"Good evening, Your Highness," he droned. "Does His Majesty—"

"Know I'm out and about? Of course he does; do you think the king stupid?"

"No, Highness! Of course not!"

"Good. Now listen up: did you see which way the mercenaries went?"

The guard hesitated, scratching his grubby bristles with an equally grubby forefinger.

"Your suitors, Highness?"

Susti muttered something under her breath, then with a wry smile, added, "Yes, that's right."

"Indeed, Your Highness; I observed their passage with the marvelous and intricate telescopic device your father was kind enough to provi—"

"Yes, yes! Which way did they go?"

The guard licked his soggy lips. "Um . . . I don't know who you mean, Your Highness," he said.

"The mercenaries!"

"W-w-which ones, Your Highness?"

Susti grimaced. "Don't play games with me, you insolent fool! My father will have you"—she paused, trying to think of the worst punishment she'd ever heard her father's chief torturer refer to—"castrapitricollapulated."

The guard's eyes practically bulged out of his head, and he began to talk very fast.

"They were heading for Rintintetly, Highness. You'll never catch them, though. Once you get into those hills, Highness, there's any one of a hundred ways you could go to get across the Washin."

"Hmm . . . Rintintetly, eh?"

"Yes, Highness. But please don't go—you'll die! They *eat* women like you in the dead city; eat 'em alive! I don't know anything else, Highness. Please don't castrapitricollapulate me!"

The man promptly folded up and sank onto his knees, but Susti wasn't paying attention to his whines. Instead, she was staring at Bronwyn with a look of sheer horror on her face.

"Everything all right, ma'am?" asked the servant,

approaching her mistress with the horses trailing behind her.

"We need to move fast, Bronny!" Susti exclaimed, snatching one of the reins and thrusting herself up into the saddle. "They must be quite a way ahead."

She watched impatiently as the servant tried and failed to get into the saddle. However, the girl's fifth attempt proved successful.

"Good. Let's go."

Bronwyn gave an impassive shrug. "I don't rightly know that we should, ma'am," she said. "The king would be terribly worried about you."

"Well, he should have thought about that before using me as an instrument of—of—of destruction!"

Susti waved her hand, and the two girls urged their horses into a healthy gallop.

"You know something really strange. . . ." Gordo muttered, as the innkeeper's geriatric nag pulled their cart along the dusty track.

"Yeah," rumbled his companion. "Moffs dunt die."

Gordo shook his head. "No, I—what did you just say?"

Groan shrugged. "Moffs, they don' die."

"Moths? What, as in ugly butt'flies?"

"Yeah."

"Don't talk rubbish."

"I'm not; bloke in the pub tol' me."

"And you believed him?"

"Yeah."

"You silly sod."

"No, I ain't. He dun proved it an' all; he jumped off a cliff wearin' a jacket made o' moff skins, and you know what 'appened?"

"Surprise me."

"He bounced."

Gordo rolled his eyes. "Is this the same bloke who told you that mohair comes from a tiny creature called a 'moe'?"

"That was TRUE! He was fightin' 'gainst all them teddy bear makers what steals the fur off 'em. That's why you see loads o' bald moes when you're out 'untin' bear fur."

Gordo smiled at his friend. "Groan, there is no such thing as a bloody 'moe'. Mohair comes from goats."

"Does it 'ell."

"Look, I'm not getting drawn into a debate over it. If you want to pay five crowns for a moth-skin coat, then that's your own lookout—"

"How did you know 'bout that?"

"I guessed."

They rode in silence for a while, then Gordo glanced over his shoulder. Gape was fast sleep in the back of the cart, and their prisoner was roped up and running along behind it.

Gordo sighed. "I can't believe we've ended up capturing Mad Count Craven's nephew," he said. "I mean, what are the odds?"

"Yeah."

The dwarf sighed again. "Come to that, I can't believe anyone can run while they're asleep," he said. "Amazing, isn't it?"

"Maybe he's dreamin' o' runnin'," said Groan.

Gordo admired the simplicity of this, and nodded. "You could be right, there. Still, brings me back to what I was going to tell you earlier. . . ."

"Yeah? What wazzat?"

"Well," the dwarf began, passing the reins to Groan, "when I checked that he was breathing, a while back, I opened his eyelids . . . and he's got one white eye and one black eye."

"Yeah," Groan rumbled, 'an' he'll 'ave two black eyes if he—"

"No, *seriously*," Gordo protested. "One white eye and one black eye. That's a mark of something; I just can't remember what. . . ."

Groan sniffed. "Who cares?"

"We might," said Gordo. "If only I could think why. . . ."

Loogie Lambontroff woke up *running*.

He managed to glance around at the landscape as it rose and fell in a swirl of eerie circles, then he lapsed into half consciousness while his mind came to terms with a few irrefutable facts. The thought process went something like:

I'm half asleep. . . .

That's because we were knocked out.

I've been captured. . . .

Yes, we're prisoners.

I'm running.

We shouldn't be.

I know I shouldn't be, but. . . . Hang on a minute. . . . Who's this *we* I keep thinking about? There is only me.

You'll remember soon. For now, why don't we find out why we're running? I mean, are we running to something or away from something?

Loogie forced open an eyelid, and promptly shut it again. His mind raced:

We're, I mean *I* am running *behind* something. I think it's a cart. What should we, I, do? And who are you, anyway? . . . Hello? Is there somebody else in here?

What?

I think there's somebody else in here.

What, besides us?

Who is this? And why did you go quiet just then?

I didn't want to upset you.

Upset me? What're you doing in here?

I'm waiting.

Waiting for what?

For you . . . to get annoyed. We both know what you're like when you get annoyed. . . . People die.

Both? There's two of you in here?

No, I meant you and I, the two of US. You are a twinling, Loogie, remember? And I am your wrath; I am the bad side of you that always surfaces when you are at your most enraged. I am your dark brother. . . .

Oh, it's YOU. I haven't seen you for ages.

Yes, Loogie, it's been a while. My, my, you haven't been this angry for a long time—must be all that medication they've got you on. Still, you seem enraged enough now, so when you're quite ready . . .

"Yeeeaaaaaaaahhhhhhhhhhh!!!"

The scream echoed through the mountains. It was so abrupt and so monstrously loud that the half-knackered horse immediately bolted forward, wrenching the reins from Groan's tight-fisted grip. The huge barbarian dived forward to snatch hold of them, which turned out to be a big mistake.

Gordo looked on in amazement as his friend was dragged, like a child's dolly, behind the bolting horse, and disappeared in the nearby woods. Then the cart fell to pieces where it stood, and Gape rolled out, his face a mixture of sleep and bewilderment.

Gordo snatched up his axe and clambered out of the woodpile, screaming all kinds of abuse about innkeepers and their wives, before focusing his attention on the source of the scream. He spun around, battle-axe at the ready, and began: "Okay, my lad, now you're in for—"

Gordo Goldeaxe froze.

"GROAAAAAANNNNN!" he boomed, taking a few steps back and raising his axe threateningly. "You better get back here, quicksmart! This bloke's a TWINLING!"

EIGHT

ILLMOOR WAS RIFE with magical creatures. A lot depended on how willing you were to see them, but a really astute hunter, in the right place at a good hour, could see sprites, demons, werewolves, vampires, pixies, imps, and even the odd gnome. Twinlings, on the other hand, were rare. On the few occasions that they *were* encountered, any hunter worth their salt would know enough to leave well alone. Twinlings were bad news. In fact, twinlings were bad-news *headlines*.

Named and shamed by the High Priests of Legrash, twinlings were those who had, at some point in their lives, been possessed by dark spirits. Upon extraction, these spirits occasionally manifested themselves physically, erupting from the souls of their hosts to wreak demonic havoc on anyone or anything unfortunate enough to get in their way. The host, meanwhile, was left in a dream state, entirely zombified until such times as the spirit's thirst for anger had been satiated, or until it had been slain. The best way to defeat a twinling, it was rumored, was to douse its demonic form in salt and promptly set fire to it, or else deliver a fatal blow to its sensitive spinal column. However, Gordo Goldeaxe didn't know this, so he dealt with it the same way he dealt with all hostile creatures; he ran at it with a bloody great axe and hoped for the best. Unfortunately, he chose the wrong twin.

The zombie half of Loogie Lambontroff staggered mindlessly toward Gordo, hardly batting an eyelash when the dwarf took its left arm off with one swift arc of the blade. Instead, it flailed madly with its right.

Gordo dived under the appendage, managed three somersaults without injuring himself—quite a feat for a dwarf with a two-foot axe—and swung around for another strike. He didn't make it.

The gangster's evil twinling, who'd been watching the proceedings with careful amusement, suddenly pounced, securing Gordo in a viselike headlock. The dwarf dropped his axe.

"Ah, look here, the little fellow doesn't like pain, does he, Loogie?"

Gordo scrambled to free himself from the hold, but the twinling had its fingers firmly locked.

"Struggle if you will, little fellow. I can feel the breath leaving your body."

Gordo tried to swivel himself around so that he could roll his way out of the headlock, but the twinling predicted his movement and promptly stamped on his shin.

"Ahhhh! You'll die for that," the dwarf managed, digging his fingernails into the twinling's hairy arm. "Groan! Gape! Grrrrrraahhhh!"

"Loogie," commanded the twin. "Get over here and fetch me this axe. We're going to slice up the little fellow with his own weapon. Ha-ha-ha-ha-ha!"

The original half of Loogie Lambontroff was staggering around the road in a daze. Almost unconscious through blood loss, he'd managed to pick up his severed limb and was trying (with little success) to fit it back into its socket.

"Loogie," the twinling persisted, tightening its grip on Gordo's neck. "Are you listening to m—"

The sentence was abruptly cut off, along with the

creature's head, which thumped onto the ground and rolled a few feet away.

Groan Teethgrit wiped the blood off his sword, and sighed. "I've los' the 'orse."

"Never mind," said Gordo, massaging his throat. "I think we've got more important things to worry about."

He indicated the felled twinling, which suddenly burst into flames and vanished. Curiously, its grinning head remained.

"Will you look at that," muttered Gordo. "Thank the gods on high."

"Fank me," Groan reminded him. He turned to Loogie the First, who was lying facedown on the floor, completely motionless. "I reckon he's dead."

"Doubt it."

"You fink we should check?"

Gordo rolled his eyes. "Be my guest," he said. "But I wouldn't go near him in a month of Sundays."

"I'll do it now," bellowed Groan, stamping over to the body. "We ain't got *that* kind o' time to waste."

"I was being metaphorical."

"Yeah, my auntie 'ad that. She used to talk out of her arse an' all. He's still breathin'. Reckon we should leave 'im 'ere?"

Gordo shook his head. "No, we'll dress his wound and take him with us."

"Why?" Groan asked, brows mating.

The dwarf knelt down, produced a bandage from his belt pouch, and began to tie a tourniquet around the gangster's stumpy arm.

"It's something the innkeeper told me," he muttered. "I've a feeling our friend here might be of some use to us in Wemeru. Besides, if he's with us then—er—we can kill him when he wakes up."

Groan scratched his head. "Why don't we just kill 'im now?"

"You can't kill a man when he's asleep! It's immoral."

"Wass that mean?"

Gordo reclaimed his axe and swung it over his shoulder. "It basically means that—er—people will think less of you if you kill him while he's asleep."

Groan peered up and down the road. "What people?"

"Just people, you know, people in general."

"What, you?"

"No, not me. OTHER people."

"But there's nobody else 'ere."

"Yes, all right! I'm speaking metaphorically again, like your aunt! Where's Gape?"

Groan shrugged, then lumbered over to the destroyed cart and heaved some wood aside. Eventually, he announced: "He's gone."

"Fantastic," snapped Gordo bitterly. "Greatest warrior of the plains, my foot. First sign of trouble, he's off like a dog with a bum full of dynamite!"

"I'm over here!"

Both Gordo and Groan spun around, but the barbarian was nowhere in sight.

"Where?" Gordo called, rummaging through the cart wreckage himself. "I can't see you!"

"HERE!" came a second shout.

Groan lumbered across the road and paused beside a steep, grass-edged pit.

"Gape's over 'ere!" he said, as if discovering the warrior was a shock to him. "Did you fall down the 'ole?"

"Yes, good brother; your perception once again amazes me. I, as you say, *fell down the hole*."

Groan frowned. "Why?"

"Because I wanted to see how deep it was; why do you think? I toppled back, and a bone in my leg let me down!"

"Wasn't your courage bone, was it?" Gordo inquired, stepping to the fringe of the pit and glaring at the warrior.

Gape returned the glare. "Listen, midget, if I had known what I was doing, I'd have creamed that damn whatever-it-was tenfold. Unfortunately, I was under the influence of sleep, and a collapsing coach cart isn't the best of circumstances in which to wake up!"

"Yeah, yeah, a likely story."

Gordo and Groan reached into the pit and helped Gape to climb out. As the warrior dusted himself off, Groan snatched up Loogie and flung him over one shoulder.

"Oi," he called back. "One o' you can bring 'is arm. I ain't carryin' it."

Pegrand Marshall blundered along the drafty corridors of Phlegm Keep's east wing and half tripped, half fell through the doors of the great library. He was carrying a bundle of scrolls.

"I'm afraid the plan's gone arse up already, milord!" he gasped. "Total bloody disaster, in fact."

Duke Modeset rolled his eyes. "Calm yourself, Pegrand," he said. "I'm sure you're overexaggerating." He closed the volume he'd been reading and flexed his fingers. "Now, take two deep breaths and *explain* the problem."

"Yes, milord." The manservant made a show of inhaling some of the room's stale air, then coughed it out again. "I've just had an urgent report, milord; the king's messenger took it from one of the guards at the front gate. Teethgrit and his band are heading for the jungles of Rintintetly, as you said they would. . . ."

Modeset looked confused. "And?"

"And the king's daughter's gone missing with one of her maids."

"So?"

"So, King Phew says that he had to tell her about your plan, and he thinks she might have gone to warn them, being the rebellious sort and all. . . ."

Modeset shook his head and pinched the bridge of his nose. Then he said, "Excuse me a moment," and disappeared into a nearby corridor.

Pegrand heard some appalling curse words before the duke reappeared and took his seat once more.

"Right," said Modeset eventually. "First things first: I want an updated and detailed description of both the princess and her maid posted on militia message boards throughout Illmoor."

"Yes, milord. Right away, milord."

"Be sure to include everything: the clothes they're wearing, hairstyles, blemishes, the lot!"

"What should I tell the king, milord?"

Modeset sighed. "Tell him to stay put. I don't want hordes of guards blundering across the countryside. If you want something done properly, you do it yourself."

"Right, milord."

"I mean it, Pegrand. I'm not taking any chances on this one. If the princess reaches Teethgrit and warns him of our plans, she'll ruin everything! Phlegm, Spittle, Dullitch, and Legrash will suffer perpetual raids from that scumbag, and I'll have made an enemy for life! So we're going to take decisive action, Pegrand, VERY decisive action. I'm going to fetch some pistols. You get the coach, and tell King Phew we're going after his daughter."

NINE

SUSTI REINED IN the horse they'd stolen from her father's stable, and motioned to Bronwyn to do the same.

"What is it, ma'am?" the servant inquired, peering along the misty road. They'd traveled a fair way from Phlegm, and were heading steadily toward the distant sound of the river.

Susti put a finger to her lips. "Trouble up ahead," she confirmed, climbing down from her ride.

"Really? How can you tell?"

"I've got a sixth sense for these things, Bronwyn."

"You mean, like in the kitchen, ma'am?"

"Don't be flippant, Bronwyn. I *do* have a sixth sense. It's just that, for some reason, it doesn't seem to work against my father."

"I see, ma'am. What do you think it is?"

"I don't know, but I'm pretty sure it's not Teethgrit's mob."

Bronwyn peered ahead, but could see only mist.

"What do you want me to do, ma'am?"

Susti flicked back her hair and pursed her lips. "Get off your horse," she said, "but keep hold of the reins, and—here—take mine, too. We're going to arrange a little ambush."

Brownwyn nervously accepted the tethers for Susti's horse. She looked exceptionally wary of the whole situation, especially when Susti made a beeline for the woods at the side of the road.

"Ma'am?"

"It's okay, Bron. I'm going into the undergrowth. I want you to count to ten, then slap both horses on the rump, and follow me. Bring some rope and a frying pan from the pack."

"But, ma'am—"

"Don't worry! I know what I'm doing." Susti flashed a demonic smile and hurried off between the trees.

A few minutes later, the maid slapped both horses hard on the rump and followed her. Together, they dashed through the undergrowth, leaping bushes, ducking low branches, and darting behind trees each time they heard a noise. At length, they reached a thickly wooded grove boasting several well-placed trees that all commanded a good view of the road. Susti was about to climb into one, when she noticed that a skinny, scruffy-looking native had beaten her to it.

"Shhh!" She motioned to Bronwyn for silence, pointing away, and whispered: "Over there, in the trees: a man."

Bronwyn followed her gaze and nodded.

After Susti had dragged her into a nearby bush, Bronwyn mouthed, "What should we do, milady?"

The princess poked her head out of their impromptu hiding place, made a quick and all-encompassing study of the area, and crouched down again.

"He looks wild," she said nervously. "Some sort of tribesman, I'm guessing. The horses have slowed, and they're wandering around on the road. He's watching them; probably waiting to ambush. I thought it was bandits, but he looks like he'd probably *eat* them. Either way, he's going to get a big surprise—"

"Well, if you say so, Majesty—"

"I do. Now listen: I'm going to climb up into the next tree and sneak up behind him. Then I'm going to crack him over the head with this frying pan. What I want *you* to do—when I give the signal—is to reach up into the tree, grab hold of his leg, and pull."

Bronwyn looked confused. "Um—what's the signal, Majesty?"

Susti thought for a moment. "This," she said, holding up a hand and making the shape of a rabbit head with her fingers. "Got it?"

"Yes, Majesty."

"Good. Let's go."

Susti took the frying pan from Bronwyn and, crawling on all fours, began to advance toward the occupied tree.

Halfway across the forest floor, she lowered herself onto her stomach and employed her elbows to work her way along.

Bronwyn gained a new respect for her mistress when she saw the princess arrive at the designated tree and climb dexterously into it, raising herself up through the branches like a native.

At length, Susti emerged onto a thick branch right behind the tree's occupant, who was carefully watching the road. He had a wiry frame, wore ragged skins, and had a rough thatch of curly black hair.

Susti raised her frying pan with one hand, then peered through the undergrowth toward Bronwyn and made the sign of the rabbit with the other.

The servant hurried up to the tree, trying her best to match her mistress's stealth, and reached a point just below the wildman's hideout.

"Now!" screamed Susti.

She brought the frying pan down hard and glanced a blow off the wildman's head, just as Bronwyn reached up and yanked at his leg. . . .

The royal coach rattled between the trees, its rickety frame threatening to retire every inch of the way.

Pegrand Marshall swore under his breath. The horse had slowed to a reluctant trot, and the thick canopy of trees occupying either side of the road looked decidedly unwelcoming. Now, to cap it all off, Modeset had ordered them into the woods.

"Are you sure about this, milord?" Pegrand called. He reined in the horse and peered back toward the coach window, where the duke's head was emerging.

"The warriors are heading for Rintintetly,

Pegrand, and we know that the princess is following them. Therefore, if we take a shortcut through these trees, we should be able to cut her off before she gets anywhere near the river. Savvy?"

"Yes, milord. Right you are, milord."

He urged the horse onward.

The Teethgrit party reached the edge of the River Washin without further incident, and Gordo breathed a huge sigh of relief when he saw a jetty stretching out over the fast-flowing waters. There was a small rowboat moored next to it.

At first, Gordo took the boat to be empty. Then Groan pointed out a bundle of rags in the bottom of it, and Gape pointed out that the rags were breathing.

Gordo trundled to the edge of the jetty and, peering into the boat for a closer look, saw the oldest man he had ever seen in his life: there were creases in every crumple, and crumples in every crease.

"Morning," it said, forcing out both syllables with terrible effort.

"Hello," said Gordo, in what he hoped was a cheerful voice. "How much to get across?"

The old man shrugged. "It's free."

"I beg your pardon?"

"What did he say?" Gape asked, crouching down to get a better view of the boat.

"He said we can go 'cross for nuffin," said Groan, who never missed an opportunity to get something for free.

"There's no charge AT ALL?" Gordo asked doubtfully.

"None," the old man assured him wearily. "We're funded by the Riverboat Association; there is no charge whatsoever for crossing these waters."

"But I thought the Riverboat Association were a load of mischievous, troublemaking deviants," Gape muttered.

The old man rolled his eyes. "Well," he said, "you learn something new every day, don't you? Now, just take a seat on the jetty and listen very carefully."

Gordo looked back at the others, then returned his attention to the boatman. "What for?" he inquired.

"For the riddle, of course."

"What? What riddle?"

"The riddle you have to answer before I can ferry you across!"

"You said it was free!"

"It *is* free; you just have to answer one simple riddle, then I'll help you on your way."

"No sweat," announced Gape, plunging his swords into the boards of the jetty and folding his legs under him. "I'm brilliant at riddles."

Gordo motioned for Groan to let down the still-unconscious Loogie Lambontroff, and they both took their ease on the jetty.

Gape laid a hand on the dwarf's shoulder. "Worry not, little friend," he whispered. "There's never been a riddle Gape Teethgrit couldn't solve."

"Yeah, right. . . ."

"I'm telling you straight, Gordo; whatever it is, I'll answer it." He turned to the boatman. "We're ready to rumble. Fire away!"

The old man yawned a few times and cleared his throat. "Right," he began. "There's this blacksmith, and he's called Pete . . ."

Gape muttered the name under his breath, a confident smile playing on his lips.

". . . and each day, Pete goes to work in the forge. On Monday, he works from nine to ten, with a ten-minute break; from ten to eleven, with a twenty-minute break; and from eleven to twelve, with a thirty-minute break. He leaves at noon. On

Tuesday, he works from nine to ten, with a five-minute break; from ten to eleven, with a fifteen-minute break; from eleven to twelve, with a thirty-minute break."

"Leaves at noon," muttered Gape, his smile slightly withered but his confidence evidently unshaken.

"Now," the old man continued, "he works six days a week, this blacksmith. On Wednesday, he follows his Monday routine; on Thursday, he follows his Tuesday routine; on Friday, his Monday routine; and on Saturday, his Tuesday one. So, on Wednesday, just after his second break, he comes into the forge . . . and a skunk's eaten his lunch. Why?"

There followed a desperately long silence, during which Loogie Lambontroff finally woke up.

A forceful gale was making the woods a lonely place, ushering carpets of leaves along dusty paths and conspiring with bark hollows to produce some decidedly unnerving noises. Thankfully, this was soon replaced by the sound of snapping twigs, as Pegrand Marshall tightened his grip on the reins and urged the horse onward.

The coach went over a rough bump in the road, and Pegrand had to grab the edge of his seat to keep his balance.

"Sorry about that, milord!" he shouted.

The carriage crashed forward, bending branches and breaking bracken. He risked a glance back over the roof of the coach at a shrieking cacophony that had been building for the last few minutes. It turned out to be the result of a frenzied fight between two squirrels and some poor relative of the gerbil that had succeeded in pinching a nut and would be dragged to hell before it would let go of it. At some point during the struggle, they must have fallen out of a tree and landed on the coach. Pegrand tried to frighten them off with a wave of his whip, but they just carried on regardless.

"How much farther to go before we're clear of these woods, milord?" he yelled, but there was no reply.

An owl swooped from the trees and settled on his shoulder, feigning affection while keeping half an eye on the little war in case the gerbil lost. Pegrand shrugged it off.

"ARE YOU ALL RIGHT IN THERE, MILORD?" he yelled.

"What?" said Modeset, his head appearing from the coach door.

Pegrand's reply was lost in the howling wind, which had picked up speed and was reaching critical proportions.

Modeset couldn't believe the strength of the gale. He put one hand to his hair and found a center parting; diagonally.

"Head east, Pegrand!" he screamed. "This is a fringe wind. It'll die away if we go deeper into the woods! And hurry up. We can't be that far behind the girl!"

Pegrand yanked on one side of the reins, and the horse jerked to the right. They thundered down a deep slope that dropped between a series of thick oaks before rising again sharply a few yards away. The wind had almost completely died away, and the trees were beginning to thin out, allowing greater light to filter through.

"Go right again!" Modeset shouted.

"Are you sure, milord?"

"Just do as you're told, damn it! I can see movement!"

TEN

"GAPE! LET GO of him, do you hear me? GAAAPE!"

Gordo snatched at the warrior's belt, his feet scraping on the jetty as he tried to stop Gape Teethgrit's advance. The barbarian had the old man hoisted high above his head, and was about to hurl him toward the rushing waters of the Washin.

"He did it on purpose," Gape said, between clenched teeth. "He purposely asked us a riddle that's impossible to answer."

"Of course he did!" Gordo yelled. "He works for the bloody Riverboat Association. They're all nuts!"

"Yeah, well, now this sticky-fingered old loon's gonna get his!"

"Don't! Please! I can't swim!" the old man cried.

The barbarian strode to the edge of the jetty and

threw the old man into the air, as if he were hurling a rag doll. There followed a long, drawn-out scream, a very big splash, and some despicable language.

"Wh-where am I?" said Loogie Lambontroff, struggling to get to his feet and staring around with a baffled expression. "Who are you people? And what's happened to my arm?"

"I'm Groan Teethgrit," said Groan, who could only deal with one question at a time. "That man what just frew the uvver man in the river is me bruvver, Gape, and the dwarf as tried to stop 'im is me partner, Gordo Gordeaxe. You're an 'ostage."

Loogie's lack of panic was startling. "What happened to my arm?" he repeated.

Groan shrugged. "We cut it off."

"A creature came out of you and tried to do us in," Gordo added, feeling that Groan's black-and-white version was a little too harsh for the gangster. "A twinling."

"Did you kill it?"

"Yes."

"Oh, thank the gods for that!" Loogie breathed a big sigh of relief. "You had me worried there for a second."

Gordo squinted at him. "We still cut your arm off," he pointed out.

"Oh yeah, I know, but it'll grow back." He thrust his remaining hand into a hidden pocket at the back of his britches and produced a flintlock pistol, which he pointed at Gordo. "Besides," he said, "I never sweat the small stuff. Get over to the end of the jetty."

"Grahnfgfffghhout!"

"Hold on, Bronny. I'm coming!"

Susti leaped down from the tree, hauled the body of the unconscious wildman off the servant, and helped her to her feet.

"He fell on top of me, ma'am."

"Yes, Bronny, couldn't be avoided I'm afraid. Now, let's unstrap this water jug thingy he's got around his waist, then we can tie him to the tree."

"Yes, ma'am."

The two girls roped the stranger to the tree, Susti tying the knot until she was satisfied that it was suitably unshakable. This done, she marched around to the front of the tree, unscrewed the wildman's water bottle, and sloshed the contents all over him.

"Ahhwhathappenedwhereami?" he spluttered, a look of absolute terror on his face.

"You're tied to a tree," said Susti, suddenly embarrassed at the stupidity of her statement. "And I want you to answer some questions before I'll even consider letting you go."

"All right, I'm game," said the captive, grinning madly.

"Good. Okay. Were you after the horses?"

"Um . . . no."

"Were you after us?"

"No."

"Then why were you going to ambush us?"

"I wasn't. I was trying to get away from something that had ambushed *me*."

Susti glanced at Bronwyn, whose concerned expression did little for her own doubts.

"In that case, why were you watching the road?"

"The thing that was after me *came* from the road."

"I see," Susti lied. "And what was it?"

"A blue tiger, I think: teeth like a shark's."

Susti peered around the grove, suddenly afraid. "That's . . . er . . . that's about all the questions I've got. Can you think of one, Bronny?"

"What do you do for a living?" asked the servant sheepishly.

"I walk."

Susti looked him up and down. "You walk?"

"Yeah."

"And you make a living from that, do you?"

"Yeah."

"But walking isn't profitable!"

He sniffed. "It is when you walk through somebody else's house."

"Aha!" Susti exclaimed. "So you're a thief?"

"Well, I'm more of a free spirit than your average, down-and-dirty thief. You know, a child of nature. I just wander across the land, meeting people and taking whatever I fancy."

"Yes, thank you. I get the picture. What's your name?"

"Stump," said Stump. "And either you've got the strangest-looking horse in the land, or that tiger's back."

Susti spun around just in time to see the enormous cobalt beast pounce from a narrow space between the trees. It landed in the center of the forest and padded toward them, snarling, growling, and grumbling, as only a determined predator can.

Bronwyn had frozen to the spot with fear, and even Susti found herself unable to move. Stump was having no trouble controlling *his* muscles, but his best efforts to wriggle free were being thwarted by the strength of the ropes that bound him to the tree.

"Help!" he screamed instead. "Somebody help!"

The two girls said and did nothing, as if by doing so they would slowly become invisible.

The tiger prowled back and forth before them. It was a lean beast, half-starved and desperate to satisfy its hunger. The creature it had been tracking was now immobilized and could be taken at will, but the two females looked so much more inviting. Hmm . . . which one first?

The tiger slavered over its lips.

Eeeny

Meany

Miny

Mo

It took one last look at the girls, then leaped into the air . . . and exploded.

A piece of lead shot ripped through the tiger's stomach, imbedding itself in the tree just above Stump's head. A second blast punctured the beast's neck as it landed. It lay still.

Modeset lowered both pistols and handed them across to Pegrand. Then he entered the woods.

"Ah, what fortune! If it isn't Susti, the noble princess on a quest to see every city in Illmoor decimated at the hands of mercenaries. Step away from the tree, please."

Susti stood her ground. "I don't take orders from dukes," she snapped. "I'm a princess."

"Yes," said Modeset, nodding, "and very nearly a dead one. Now *move*."

To Susti's surprise, the duke aimed the pistol at her.

"You wouldn't dare, Modeset. My father—"

"—wouldn't have a clue. Now stop being a spoiled brat and get into the coach." He turned to Bronwyn. "You too."

Susti and Bronwyn exchanged glances, then began to move toward the duke.

Pegrand pointed past Modeset's shoulder at the tree. "What about him, milord?"

"Who?"

"Over there, tied to the tree."

"Oh, good grief, is that human? I thought it was a monkey."

"His name is Stump," Susti said. "He's a no-good, down-and-dirty thief."

"Thanks a lot," said Stump as the two girls

clambered reluctantly into the duke's coach. "Any chance of letting me free, Your Majestum?"

Modeset raised an eyebrow. "Hmm . . . that depends. Why did they tie you up?"

"Tiger bait."

"Sounds reasonable. Though, by the state of you, I doubt very much that you'd have satisfied it." He motioned to Pegrand to untie the prisoner, then he climbed inside the coach and slammed the door.

"Thanks for this," said Stump cheerfully. "I really appreciate it. Of course, if it wasn't for your girls, I wouldn't be tied up in the first place, but still, live and let live."

"They're not *our* girls," Pegrand muttered, breaking the knot and gathering up the rope. "And you're a free man."

"Good stuff."

"Right."

Pegrand slung the rope over one shoulder and headed off toward the coach. He stopped halfway, and spun around. "Where are you going?"

"I'm coming with you."

"What? Get lost!"

"I need a ride."

"Forget it."

"C'mon; it wouldn't kill you, would it?"

Pegrand muttered something under his breath.

"What's the holdup?" Modeset called from the coach.

"Nothing!" the manservant replied. "Just trying to get rid of this nomad!"

"I prefer the term 'free spirit' myself."

Pegrand snatched a handful of Stump's hair and pulled him into whispering distance.

"Get on the back bar," he said. "And don't make a noise."

"You're making a big mistake, friend," said Gordo, shuffling backward in the direction of the river while Loogie advanced on him. "We never forget a face."

The gangster gave a lopsided shrug. "I don't make mistakes, and you're not my friends. Now drop your weapons and get to the edge of the jetty. ALL OF YOU."

Gordo threw down his battle-axe and reversed until he bumped into Gape, who'd turned his back on the threats of the splashing boatman to face the greater threat from the gangster. Groan, on the other hand, hadn't moved an inch.

"AND YOU." Loogie leveled the pistol at

Groan, his grin melting away. "MOVE YER BONES."

Groan spat on the gangster's boots. "Make me."

"I beg your pardon?"

"You 'erd."

"Don't be stupid, Groan!" Gordo shouted, beginning to wish he hadn't dropped his axe. "He's got a bloody pistol!"

The giant barbarian shrugged. "He looks 'armless to me. Ha-ha-ha-ha-ha!"

There was an unnerving click.

"Don't push me," Loogie muttered. "I'm *warning* you."

Groan flexed his considerable chest muscles. "C'mon then," he said. "Do ya worst."

After that, five things happened very quickly: Groan dropped onto his knees and rolled forward, his brother gave a shrill whistle, Loogie fired his pistol, Gordo dived backward into the river, and Gape's two enchanted swords shot out of the ground and decapitated the gangster.

Loogie's head toppled off his shoulders and rolled along the ground.

"Damn you to hell!" it said.

PART TWO

THE TRUTH

ELEVEN

"THIS IS RIDICULOUS," Gape said, rowing the little boat across the Washin. By some miracle (and despite the fact that the boat was obviously a two-seater), they'd all managed to cram in. Still, it was a tight squeeze, especially with Groan sprawled over the bench, fast asleep.

"What is?" Gordo muttered, sniffing miserably and wringing out his plaited beard. "If you've got something to say, why don't you just say it?"

Gape brought the oars level and allowed the water to settle. "Well," he started. "First you bring this idiot along for the ride—"

"—because of what the innkeeper told us."

"And what was that, exactly?"

Gordo rolled his eyes. "He's Craven's nephew! I thought that having him along might give us some leverage in Rintintetly!"

"Ahh, of course! But then he turned out to be some kind of creature and grew a brother—"

"Yes, as you are very well aware."

"And then you cut his arm off?"

"You know I did."

"So why have we still got his head, exactly?"

Gordo ignored Gape's thumbed reference to the bloodied bundle of cloth beside his leg, and sighed in an attempt to ebb his rising temper. "Because he's still alive! You saw him speaking!"

"I did," the warrior confirmed. "Yet I fail to see how carrying the decapitated head of Craven's long-lost nephew into Rintintetly is going to get us sufficiently on the count's good side for him to then give up his wife's wedding ring."

"Don't be funny, Gape. It doesn't suit you."

"I'm being serious, GORDO." He seized hold of the oars and began to row again, with smooth, easy strokes. After a while, he put on a silly voice and mimicked: "Lord Craven, we have traveled far to get to your fair city. We know that you are a terrible, murdering tyrant, who bathes in the blood of chickens, but we're hoping that you might take pity on us and, perchance, give us your new wife's wedding ring, in return for which we will reunite you with your long-lost nephew's . . . decapitated head. It still talks, so I'm sure you can get any outstanding family problems ironed out, and besides, if you can't, you can always use him as a football."

The silence that followed was abruptly broken by a muffled expletive from the cloth bundle. Gordo reached down, shook off the rags, and sat the head of Loogie Lambontroff on his knee.

"Unprovoked," it said. "That was completely and utterly unprovoked."

Gordo boggled at it. "You what? You shot at us, for crying out loud."

"Yeah, pity I missed. I could've been—"

"What the hell are you, anyway?" Gape interrupted. "What kind of creature stays alive when you cut its head off."

"He's a twinling."

"Er, I am," said the head. "But I'm also a zombeegol."

"What's that?"

"Part zombie, part ghoul. It means I can regenerate, given time and the right persuasion. Mind you, this is gonna put me to the test, all right."

Gordo nodded. "A zombeegol," he repeated. "It figures, considering your background. . . ."

"Ha! You're a bloody dwarf—what do you know about my background?"

"I know you're Count Craven's nephew!"

"Don't mention that name in my presence!"

"Oh, it's like that, is it?"

"Did he send you?"

Gordo shook his head. "No, we're freelance. It just so happens that we're headed for Rintintetly."

"You're not taking me there!"

"Yes we are," said Gape. "Don't argue."

"You better not."

"We *are*!" snapped Gordo. "Just accept it."

"I could make life very unpleasant for you."

"How? What're you going to do? Spit at us?"

The head was thoughtful for a time. Then it said: "Why are you going there, exactly?"

Gordo and Gape shared a glance, during which Groan almost tipped the boat over by rolling onto his side.

"We're going to steal something," the dwarf admitted. "A ring."

"Does it belong to my uncle?"

"In a manner of speaking."

"Good. In that case, I'll help you . . . for a price."

Gape burst into a fit of laughter. "You? Help? Ha-ha-ha-ha-ha-ha-ha! How, for crying out loud?"

Again, the head became thoughtful.

"I could be your lookout," it said. "You could hold me over walls, around corners, and I could tell you if there was anything coming. You know, like guards and such. I'm also very intelligent."

"Ha!" Gordo exclaimed. "You're nothing but a footpad."

"I am *now*, but before that I was privately educated. I've got a decree in astronomy, a diplodocus in archaeology, and six medals from the Dullitch Society of Treasure Hunters, where, I might add, I was president for a year. Not to mention—"

Gape sniggered, but Gordo silenced him with a well-aimed shin kick.

"You're on," said the dwarf. "What's your price?"

The head grinned. "Well, I suppose it depends. . . ."

"On?"

"Well, er, how much is it worth? You know, the thing you're planning to steal."

"It's not worth a crown," Gape said, before

Gordo could make something up. "At least, not to us. We need it because we—that is, my brother and I—are trying to woo a beautiful princess."

"And she won't wed unless we can bring her four legendary great treasures," Gordo added. "One of which happens to be the ring given to Lady Khan by your uncle."

"Ha! She was mine before she was his, you know."

"Lady Khan," Gordo repeated slowly, "was your, um, partner?"

"You could say that. We were very close."

"And now she's your auntie?"

The head screwed up its face. "Only on paper," it said finally. "Besides, I doubt whether Lady Khan'd *need* a ring."

"Why's that?"

"She's a chicken."

When Duke Modeset's coach came rattling into Phlegm, King Phew and an assortment of his royal bodyguard were waiting in the keep's courtyard.

As the assembled company looked on, the horse slowed to a trot and eventually stopped. The coach door swung open, and Susti stepped out into the light, followed by Bronwyn and, presently, Duke Modeset.

As Pegrand urged the horse into a trot and made for the stables, a lone figure slipped from the back of the coach and began to stroll nonchalantly across the courtyard.

King Phew ran up to his daughter and waggled a stubby finger at her. "I warned you not to get involved!" he snapped.

Susti merely folded her arms and scowled at him.

"You should listen to your father," Modeset advised her. "He's much older and a good deal wiser than you."

Susti turned to look at the duke and smiled grimly. "I know," she said. "He's also much older and a good deal wiser than *you*."

"I'm not *that* much older than him," said King Phew resentfully. "Besides, Lord Modeset speaks for the national community."

"I'll just bet he does."

"And what, pray tell, is that supposed to mean?" Modeset inquired.

"She's young, my friend; she doesn't know what she's talking about."

King Phew dismissed his royal bodyguard, swung an arm around his daughter's shoulders, and attempted to steer her away. He failed.

"I'll tell you what it means," Susti yelled, ducking under her father's arm and thrusting an accusing finger at Modeset. "It means that I think you've got a personal grudge against Groan Teethgrit that goes all the way back to that business in Dullitch, with the rats."

Modeset's expression went cold. "Nonsense."

"That's enough, Susti!" warned the king.

"No it isn't, Father, not nearly enough. He's used what pitiful influence he has left with the Great Assembly to drag everyone into a war on mercenaries, and you and the other rulers are all so stupid that you've fallen for it!"

The color had drained from Modeset's cheeks; his eyes were bloodshot.

"King Phew," he said. "Please remove your daughter from my face."

The king took a step forward and almost walked into the hairy monstrosity that suddenly appeared between his daughter and the duke.

"Evening, all," said Stump jovially, nodding to the group in general. "Ah, so you're a princess, are you? Ha! Good thing he didn't shoot you, then, eh?"

"How did you get here?" Modeset demanded.

"Er, I sneaked onto your coach—nifty ride, that."

King Phew glared at the duke. "You were going to shoot my daughter?"

"No, no, of course n—"

"He was too! He said you'd never know!"

Modeset suddenly thrust out a fist and struck the wildman, who stumbled backward and fell onto his behind. Stump moaned a little, then rolled over and began to crawl away in the direction of the stables.

"I'm sorry about that, Your Majesty," he said. "But I can't stand liars, especially when they *interrupt*."

King Phew didn't say anything. He was glaring at the duke with something approaching disgust.

"You threatened my daughter with a *pistol*?" he said.

Modeset sighed. "Well, she would never have climbed into the coach if I'd simply *asked* her to."

"How DARE you!"

"Now, listen to me—"

"Guards!"

"Wait just a moment."

"GUARDS!"

Two heavily armored protectors clattered down the keep steps and came to stand on either side of the duke.

Modeset held up his hands for calm. "Think very carefully, I implore you," he said, as Pegrand came strolling around the corner, stopping dead when he saw the scene unfolding at the keep steps.

"No, Duke Modeset, it is *you* who should have thought carefully before you pointed a pistol at my daughter."

Susti looked down at her feet, but couldn't stop the smile that was forming on her lips.

"King Phew," Modeset snapped. "I might remind you that I am currently Chairman of the Great Assembly."

"An honorary title," spat the king, but his voice wavered a little.

Modeset shrugged. "Honorary or not, I currently have at my disposal oaths from the combined armies of Dullitch, Legrash, and Spittle. Do you really want a war, Your Majesty?"

"Dullitch would never throw in with the likes of you; Curfew can't stand you."

The duke flashed a demonic grin. "Viscount

Curfew is family," he stated. "Besides, he's always rather liked Phlegm. It's such a . . . wealthy kingdom."

"And we've no real trainin' to speak of," said one of the guards suddenly.

Modeset turned to regard the man, and nodded an agreement. "You wouldn't stand a chance, I'm afraid."

"Guards," Phew snapped. The king was now so enraged that his face had flushed a dark red. "Arrest this man."

There was no movement. Susti looked horrified, the guards bewildered.

Modeset patted both men companionably on the shoulder. "Gentlemen, if you'd be so kind," he said in a matter-of-fact tone.

The guards took a step forward, each seizing an elbow, and hoisted King Phew into the air.

"Put me down, damn you! What is the meaning of this? I demand to be let down! I am your *king*."

Susti raised a hand to strike the nearest guard, but Pegrand rushed forward and caught hold of the princess's arm. Bronwyn made a valiant attempt to rescue her mistress, but Pegrand soon had both girls restrained. Another group of sentries arrived, alerted by the row in the courtyard. For a moment it looked as though they would side with the king, but a quick discussion with their captains dissolved any opposition to the mutiny.

"What should we do with 'em?" said the guard who had first spoken to Modeset.

The duke rubbed his chin thoughtfully. "Your name?" he inquired.

"Captain Crikey, sir."

"Well, *General* Crikey, if I were you, I'd confine them both to their respective quarters. The princess may keep her maid. After all, there's no need to be *difficult* about things, is there?"

King Phew, still angrily protesting, was dragged away. Two guards followed with Bronwyn in tow, and as Susti was brought past, Modeset grabbed her roughly by the throat.

"You're a very spirited young lady," he said. "But do be careful; I'd hate for something unfortunate to happen to you. . . ."

Susti resisted the urge to spit in the duke's face, and allowed the guards to lead her away.

"What should I be doing, milord?" Pegrand asked, peering around the courtyard as if he were disappointed that all the drama was over.

"Nothing at all, Pegrand."

Modeset allowed himself a deep and satisfying smile that was soon wiped off his face when Stump went thundering past on the royal coach, two fingers raised in frank defiance, and whistling a merry tune.

TWELVE

APPROXIMATELY halfway across the Washin, a deadly silence had descended upon the little rowboat. Groan was awake, Gape and Gordo were aghast, and all three of them were staring at the head with a certain amount of grim trepidation.

"Go on," said Gordo wearily.

The head frowned. "Where was I?"

"You were telling us about your uncle's wife . . . the chicken." Gape reminded him. "And also about the hideous army of deadlies he's got coffined up in his palace gardens."

"Yeah, right," the head continued, sniffing a little. "Well, as I was saying, Wemeru's quite a fortress. It's hidden just inside the western edge of Rintintetly."

"I wanna hear more about the chicken," Groan roared.

The head made a face. "Yes, well, I don't really want to talk about that," it snapped. "The memory is still very painful to me."

"I don't give a monkey's nut," said Groan. "Tell us, or else."

"No."

"I could make ya."

"I could bite your hand off."

"I could lob you into the lake."

"Can we stop this nonsense?" Gordo said. "It's not helping anyone. Personally, I don't give a damn about some stupid chicken."

"Seconded," Gape said, swapping places with Groan, who proceeded to row them the rest of the way. "I just want to grab the ring and get the hell out of there."

"Right," Gordo agreed. "So, Loogie, you definitely don't know anything about this ring?"

The head tried to shake itself. "Not a sausage. Mind you, I *have* been away from Wemeru for a very long time."

"Well, get ready for a big reunion, numskull." Gape laughed. "Because you're on your way back."

Modeset marched into the throne room of Phlegm

Keep, waited for Pegrand and the newly appointed General of the Guard to file in behind him, then slammed the doors loudly.

"Exactly how many troops do we have at our disposal?" he said.

General Crikey did a quick finger count. "Two hundred, sir."

"Superb! Horses?"

"Ten, sir."

"You're joking."

"No, sir. Ten horses, one broken catapult, and a cart, sir. The king never really invested in burden."

Modeset swore under his breath.

"Listen," he said. "I want you to send out a couple of soldiers after my coach."

"Why's that, milord?" his manservant asked, not noticing the duke's pained expression.

"Because it's *my* coach, Pegrand."

"It's a run-down old heap, milord."

"Yes, but it's *my* coach."

"Certainly, sir!" chirped Crikey, snapping off a smart salute. "I shall see to it immediately."

Modeset nodded. "Good man. And make sure you bring the wildman back to me; preferably breathing, but I'm not fussy."

"Yes, SIR!"

Pegrand waited until the general had departed, then leaned over toward Modeset and whispered: "Why do we want to capture Stump, milord? Surely we can just let him go. . . ."

The duke shook his head vehemently. "I don't know how that imbecile got aboard the coach without us noticing, but he just overheard that entire argument. I don't want word getting out that I've taken control of Phlegm. The other rulers . . . won't like it."

"I thought you said they'd be on your side, milord."

"Ha!" Modeset laughed at the prospect. "Dear, dear Pegrand, the lords of Spittle, Dullitch, and Legrash wouldn't so much as spit on my rotting carcass if I were engulfed by flame."

"I'm sure that's not true, milord. I mean, after all, Viscount Curfew *is* your cousin."

Modeset thought for a second, then nodded. "Yes, Pegrand, that he is. But, if you remember correctly, I had his mother beheaded."

The manservant frowned with the effort of recollection. "So you did, milord," he said eventually. "So you did. Best not to ask him for any favors then, eh?"

"You said it." Modeset climbed the steps that led to King Phew's marble throne and took his rest upon it. "Now, let's assess the situation," he said. "I've inadvertently seized a city—which is good—but I have to keep my presence here a secret—which isn't. I've also got an army—which is good—but I can't afford to let it out of my sight—which isn't. Hmm . . ."

Pegrand waited for his master to form a plan. He was used to the procedure, and counted a full twenty seconds before making a suggestion.

"How about shutting the place up, milord?"

"Mmm?"

"You know, like in a siege but without all the people outside trying to starve you out."

"Pegrand, please endeavor to make yourself clear."

"Well, milord, I'm just saying that if you shut all the gates, put guards on the outer walls, and closed the road in, then you could probably sit it out here until the cows come home."

Modeset appeared to consider this. "What about the other lords?" he questioned.

"I dunno much about that, milord. I mean, how often do they talk to each other in the normal way?"

"Hardly ever. In fact, we had to use each of them

as leverage even to get the others to turn up for the Great Assembly in Shadewell. Disgusting, isn't it?"

Pegrand nodded. "Don't you have to report to them about this Teethgrit plan of yours?"

"No, there's no need. Nobody expects them to come back! Isn't it fantastic? I've got a hold on the richest city in Illmoor, the other rulers don't have a clue, and the Teethgrits and Goldeaxe are dead meat! Ha! I can't lose, Pegrand. I'm finally winning!"

The manservant nodded cheerfully. "Yes, milord," he agreed. "So shall I tell Crikey to lock all the citizens up?"

Modeset's face dropped. "I beg your pardon?"

"Well, I doubt if they'll be pleased when they hear that you've usurped their king, milord; and if we don't want them climbing over the walls, I reckon we should probably lock 'em all up."

"What, in the dungeons?"

Pegrand shrugged. "They're big enough, aren't they?"

"But we can't do that! That's, that's tyrannical!"

"Yes, milord, but do you remember what happened in Dullitch, with the riots? If we strike now, street by street, we can probably nip things in the bud, nice and early, before the troublemakers get started."

Modeset gave a reluctant nod. "Pegrand," he said. "Once again, you're absolutely right."

It was getting dark as Gape and Groan leaped from the boat onto the eastern shore of the Washin, dragging the little vessel along behind them.

Gordo waited until he was sure the boat had firm ground beneath it, then followed. The head of Loogie Lambontroff, which was fastened to the dwarf's belt via its hair, bounced around in a rather undignified fashion.

"Go slow, can you?" it complained. "I feel like a yo-yo down here."

"Silence," Gape commanded, as he and his brother cautiously approached the western fringe of Rintintetly. The wood was practically *on* the river. "At least until we get a little way in."

The head muttered into the silence, and the group carefully proceeded.

"Wait a minute," said Gordo. "Shouldn't we camouflage the boat?"

"Why?"

"In case someone steals it!"

Gape shrugged. "I suppose," he said, and beckoned for Groan to help him. They flipped the vessel over and covered it with foliage. Then they entered the dark fringe of the wood.

An owl hooted somewhere off to the right, and various tiny creatures could be heard scurrying between the trees.

Gordo's battle-axe gleamed in the moon-light, and there was a distinct hum from Gape's enchanted blades. Even Groan's enormous broad-sword seemed unnaturally small in the terrible depths of the wood.

"Which way?" Gordo whispered to the head.

"Er, left, that's it, no, right. Hang on. Go back a ways, then turn east, no—"

"Oh, for god's sake!" Gape snapped. "You don't have the slightest clue, do you?"

"Not really, no."

"This way," Groan thundered, causing both of them to turn toward him (the head didn't have a choice).

"How do you know?"

Groan shrugged. "Smells o' death."

"Sounds promising," said Gape, creeping after his brother and signaling to Gordo to do the same.

"I can see where he's going, phlegm-ball; I don't need hand gestures."

"Shh!"

"Shh yourself!"

The trees seemed to be drawing together, bending so low that the path ahead was almost totally hidden.

"Ah, this is the way," the head advised. "I'm sure of it."

Groan took no notice, carving his way through the undergrowth with reckless abandon. Gape was creeping close behind him, swords drawn at the ready.

"Looks very familiar, this bit," the head droned on.

Gordo was feeling increasingly nervous. He'd seen something moving between the trees, and he was fairly certain that it wasn't alone. Still, he didn't want to mention it to the others until he was one hundred percent sure that the "something" was following them. Fortunately, he didn't have to wait very long to find out. An arrow zipped through the wood and plunged into a tree, three inches from Gape's right ear.

THIRTEEN

STUMP HAD MADE a startling discovery about horses. The thing that he'd found out, much to his dismay, was that you could get a horse to gallop with relative ease: it was getting it to *stop* galloping that caused the problem. In fact, the royal mare was going at such a speed that he'd briefly considered severing all links with the coach and letting the cursed thing trundle off to hell on its own. Unfortunately, the tethers were fastened far too well to disengage while the horse was in motion. Stump cursed under his breath, and clung on to the reins for dear life.

To make things worse, there were a couple of soldiers after him. He could hear them thundering along a short distance behind him, and it sounded as though they had stronger horses than the crazy beast he'd stolen. They were definitely gaining on him.

Stump grimaced.

He was over the last of the hills now, and there was a river coming up. It slid along below him like a watery serpent.

"Stop! Stop! Please stop!" he screamed, thrashing the reins with all his might, which only served to make the horse go faster. He dived below the bench and made one final attempt to disconnect the coach, his fumbling fingers straining at a concealed lever beneath the rein hooks. There was a tiny click and, to Stump's surprise, the horse galloped a little to the right, about-turned, and gently clip-clopped to a halt. Unfortunately, the coach didn't. . . .

Stump cried out as the severed vehicle careered down the embankment and plunged into the icy waters of the Washin.

A solitary old man watched from the near bank, cackling cruelly when he saw the frantic stranger clambering onto the roof of the coach as it sank into the water. He found the whole scene very entertaining; it was only a pity his *own* boat had gone.

There came the sudden and unmistakable sound of hoofbeats, and two horses exploded down the hill toward the river. They soon slowed, and the soldiers mounted on them dropped to the ground and began to draw crossbows from their saddlebags.

The old man chuckled with delight as they began to fire on the stranger, who, by this time, was quite a way out on the river, balancing precariously on the roof of the half-submerged coach, with both hands covering his head.

The crossbows spewed their bolts at the coach, obliterating various parts of the coach roof but mercilessly missing the man struggling madly for purchase atop it.

"Stolen your coach, has he?" the old man screamed at the soldiers. "Get him; go on! Bloody thieves! They're all scum!"

Their first rounds spent, the soldiers paused to reload their weapons. When they looked up again, their target had disappeared.

"Down! Down! DOWN!"

Gape threw himself to the floor, and Groan stepped behind a sturdy oak as the arrows flew hard and fast through the trees. Gordo, on the other hand, hefted his battle-axe in both hands and dashed forward, the head bouncing up and down at his waist.

"Get back here, you crazy midget!" Gape yelled, but the dwarf was already accelerating away from the path at top speed.

"I can handle it! I can handle it!" Gordo called back, his battle-axe visible every few seconds in brief flashes.

There was a series of screams, a few low moans, and then the arrows stopped coming.

Groan stepped out from behind his tree, and Gape jumped to his feet.

The forest was completely silent.

Then a scream started up, low at first, but quickly increasing in pitch . . .

. . . and Gordo Goldeaxe came rushing back into view, the head a veritable blur on his belt. It was screaming: "He can't handle it! He can't handle it!"

A line of figures appeared between the trees. Several were staggering around in the daze of the living dead, while a few leveled long bows from afar. There was a moment of grim realization before the arrows started up again, exploding all over the wood like rogue fireworks.

Groan stepped forward, ducked two arrows, and pitched his sword at the nearest figure. The giant blade arced through the air and sprouted out of the first unfortunate like a third arm. The zombie in question staggered back, then casually removed the sword and tossed it aside like an unwanted Christmas present.

Gape was next to be disappointed. His enchanted swords met their mark, but were soon retrieved and discarded by the dauntless zombies.

Gordo, however, was having more luck. He'd quickly decided that the bowmen were the more immediate threat, and had acted accordingly, putting one down with his belt dagger, beheading the second with his axe, and knocking the third out cold with a well-aimed blow to the head (or rather, a well-aimed blow *with* the head). At least, he reflected as he bent down to retrieve Loogie's moaning cranium, he'd managed to stop the arrows.

Groan and Gape were physically fighting the first of the zombies to reach them: Gape with a series of kicks and punches, and Groan by using one of the zombies to bowl out the two behind it. However, the sheer weight of numbers prevailed, and the two barbarians were quickly overwhelmed.

Gordo fought on, lopping off arms and legs left, right, and center. Unfortunately, for every limb that he severed, another quickly sprang up to take its place.

"How come you haven't regenerated so quickly?" he barked at the head of Loogie Lambontroff, stepping back with his axe held aloft as the zombies advanced.

"It's the twinling thing," Loogie snapped. "Takes a lot out of me."

"Typical," Gordo managed, swinging wide. "I don't suppose you could make it happen again, could you?"

"Nah, sorry," the head muttered. "Only happens when I least expect it. Besides, I doubt an evil head would do you much good in these circumstances."

"Good point."

"No, I was joking. I don't reckon my physical state would have any bearing on the *other* me: not if I got *really* mad—"

Gordo took another wild swipe at the zombies, but this time one caught hold of the axe head and wrenched it from the dwarf's grasp. Another lumbered at Gordo, seizing him around the neck, while a third snatched up his legs. He was carried along the path in this curiously undignified fashion, noticing as he went that the others were being conveyed similarly. A stout zombie with matted black hair was leading the group, while a pale and particularly gaunt one at the back of the group carried their weapons.

"They're taking us to Wemeru," the head whispered.

Gordo twisted and turned in the zombies' grip. "But you're the nephew of their lord," he spat. "Can't you order them to let us go?"

"I'm disgraced," Loogie explained. "And you can understand them not recognizing me, all things considered."

Gordo conceded the point. It really was turning out to be one of those days again.

"Does Modeset know you're doing this?" Susti asked, when Pegrand arrived at her chamber door with two giant platters of food.

The manservant nodded. "Yes, milady. In fact, I'm bringing you these under the duke's instructions."

"Ha! Then they're probably poisoned."

Pegrand shook his head.

"Oh, no, milady. Duke Modeset would never knowingly do you harm."

"Ha! Don't be ridiculous; didn't you hear him threaten me earlier?"

"Oh, well, Duke Modeset threatens *everyone*; he's just not very good at following things through."

Susti grimaced. "Well he's certainly done all right for himself here, hasn't he?" she snapped.

Pegrand didn't reply. He simply laid down both platters on the room's single table and took a step back.

Bronwyn jumped up from the corner of the bed on which she'd been perched, hurried across the room, and began to tuck into the food. She was ravenously hungry.

Susti, it seemed, was in no such hurry.

"Have you worked for him long?" she asked, looking the scruffy manservant up and down with a disdainful glance.

Pegrand shrugged. "Since I was six."

"And now you're . . . ?"

"Thirty-nine."

"Really? Have you had a very hard life?"

"Not particularly, milady."

"Only, you look a lot older."

"Thank you, milady; very kind of you to say so."

"Hmm . . . so you were with him during the rat catastrophe?"

Pegrand nodded. "Yes, milady. I was also with

him when he saved the city from a fanatical cult, at no small risk to his own safety."

Susti took exception to the manservant's tone, but smiled in spite of herself. "You really like him, don't you?"

"He's my master," said Pegrand. "I have to!"

"No, you don't," Susti assured him. "You don't *have* to like anybody!"

Pegrand shrugged, and turned to watch Bronwyn hungrily devouring the remains of a pork chop. At length, he returned his attention to the young princess.

"How old are you, milady?" he ventured. "If it's not a rude question."

"I'm eighteen," said Susti cautiously. "Why?"

Pegrand smiled. "Well, speaking as someone more than twice your age, I believe that Duke Modeset is a good man. A little unpredictable, maybe, but good nonetheless."

"What does age have to do with it?"

"I'm just saying that I probably know more about people than you do, milady."

Susti chuckled. "That's the biggest load of nonsense I've ever heard in my life. You're a manservant to a man who has probably, in his lifetime, been responsible for more chaos than any other single man in the history of the continent. You do realize that, don't you?"

Pegrand quickly shook his head. "I'm afraid you're wrong. Duke Modeset *is* a good person, he just *needs* to be in charge of a city. If he's not, he gets . . . touchy."

"Touchy?" Susti exclaimed. "Touchy? He's imprisoned my father and taken control of the city guard!"

"Look, I don't want to argue with you, milady. Apart from anything else, you're a princess, and it's not my place."

The manservant headed for the door, and was halfway through it when Susti called him back.

"Yes, milady?"

"You seem like a decent fellow, Pegrand," she said. "And if you ever see sense long enough to dump Duke Modeset, I'm sure there would be a job for you in Phlegm."

Pegrand considered this, but politely declined. "I already have a job in Phlegm, milady," he said. "I work for the duke."

FOURTEEN

STUMP was progressing through the Washin via a series of dives and breathers, turning over and over as he struggled against the flow of the river.

Every now and then, a bolt would explode far behind him; a grim reminder that certain death (or at least, inescapable injury) waited for him above the waters. With this in mind, he dived deeper, letting more and more time pass before he came up for air.

At length, he began to drift into a swoon, and the water took him. He washed up, some two hours later, on the eastern bank of the Washin; a sodden, bedraggled mess, but cleaner than he had been for years.

Far behind him, the Phlegmian guards had remounted their horses and were attempting to wade their way out to the coach. However, it soon became clear that the water was too high for this procedure, and they had to turn back, tether up the horses, and swim to the coach instead.

The first man to reach it clambered atop the vehicle roof, which was now almost totally submerged beneath the waters. There was no sign of their target.

"He's not here!" the guard called back to his partner, who nodded and dived underwater in order to search the sunken coach. After about thirty seconds, he reappeared.

"Nothing!" he shouted. "Maybe he drowned?"

The first guard produced a miniature telescope from his belt and attempted to study the far shore.

"See anything?"

"Nah, it's too dark."

"Maybe we should camp here; look again in the morning. . . ."

"Ha! Are you serious? Let's just tell the general he drowned and have done with it."

The first guard looked doubtful. "General said to bring him in dead or alive," he said. "Besides, I reckon he'll make us come back for the coach."

The second guard shrugged. "Crikey's only been

a general since yesterday, and besides, if he's *that* keen on the coach, he can send a squad out for it."

"Yeah, right."

They made one final search of the waters around the coach's periphery, and began to head back to the shore.

When they got there, an elderly man was waiting for them, his face creased with smiles.

"You two aren't up to much, are ya?" he cackled.

The guards, soaking wet and in no mood for banter, ignored him and marched on past.

"Oi! Come back here! He got away, you know!"

They stopped, and one turned around.

"Say that again, old-timer?"

The old man pointed out at the river. "Your boy in the coach," he confirmed. "Swam for it, sure as I was sitting here watching."

The guards glanced at each other.

"Is there anyone else around here?" one inquired.

"No, not a soul. I'm only here because I work for the Riverboat Association. At least, I did until a gang of bloody barbarians took my boa—"

A crossbow bolt fired at point-blank range cut short the old man's words, and he collapsed to the ground.

"I dunno," said the first guard. "It's nothing but work, work, work, isn't it?"

His partner sniggered, and the two of them mounted their horses and rode away.

As Groan, Gordo, and Gape were led deeper into the woods by Count Craven's zombie horde, the city of Wemeru came into view. It wasn't a pretty sight, even in the fading light.

An avenue of hulking temples swept away from the entrance, and various smaller, pyramidal dwellings were visible in between them. Everything that wasn't covered in hanging vines was smothered in mud. The entire place reeked of death and decrepitude.

"No place like home," Loogie muttered from the dwarf's belt. Gordo wondered if he was serious.

The zombies were leading them toward an enormous, central pyramid that rose about a hundred feet above the temples surrounding it. A rough wooden sign dug into the dirt proclaimed it to be:

H'eylr
The Great House of Wemeru

Gordo took a deep breath: if the air in the streets smelled like this, he had absolutely no desire to see inside *this* pyramid. Gape was experiencing a similar sense of disgust, and couldn't quite believe his ears when his brother sauntered past, whistling.

Count Elias Craven got up twice a year.

There were many reasons for this; most of them having to do with the fact that the ruler of Wemeru existed on very little blood, could barely stand up most of the time, and was about as far past death as any animate creature was ever likely to get. He was also a necromancer, and many people said that the main reason he remained so fast asleep was that no bugger in their right mind would ever dare to wake him.

Well, someone was waking him now. He could hear the giant coffin lid being hefted off.

Torchlight streamed in: burning, blinding torchlight. Still, it could've been worse—they could've woken him during the day.

Count Craven opened an eye, but there were cobwebs in his socket, and he realized he'd opened the wrong one. He soon corrected that, and a bloodred pupil considered the trembling figure of his zombie captain.

"Well?"

"Intruders, master."

"I find that very difficult to believe."

"I'm serious, master; we've caught some intruders."

"I thought I told you to stop hunting on the Washin. The corpse pit is chockablock!"

"We didn't hunt these, master. They were heading *into* the wood."

"Don't be stupid. No one in their right mind would enter Rintintetly from this side of the wood."

"Nevertheless, master, *these* did."

Count Craven rolled his good eye, raised himself up, and clambered out of the coffin.

"How many?" he snapped.

"Three, master: two large warriors and a dwarf."

"Bring the men to me."

"And the dwarf, master?"

"Drown him."

"Yes, master."

As the zombie captain juddered away, Count Craven pulled himself together: literally.

Then he staggered out of the family crypt and began the long haul to the throne room (when every breath's an effort, twelve feet can be an awfully long way away).

The entire surviving citizenry of Wemeru—which amounted to approximately twenty zombies—awaited him there, tottering around on their fractured legs like a group of oversized penguins. There was a succession of low, brainless muttering, and the Teethgrits were shoved to the front. A small space cleared around them as Count Craven slumped onto his wicker throne.

"What do you want in Wemeru?" he began, each word sounding as though it had been scoured with sandpaper.

"We've come for Lady Khan's ring," Gape announced pompously.

"Yeah," Groan added. "An' we're not goin' wivout it!"

Count Craven gave this a moment's consideration; it took three quarters of an hour.

"Lady Khan," he said, as though the two men that stood before him were stark-raving mad, "is a chicken. And no one leaves Wemeru alive."

"It's funny you should say that," Gape said, beginning to untie the makeshift knot around his wrists. "Because, unless you hand over the ring, we're not going to leave anyone *in* Wemeru alive."

"Interesting," muttered Craven, biting at what was left of his lower lip. "I've never been threatened before—"

"—and you'll never be threatened again," Gape finished, breaking the knot but keeping both hands behind his back. "I guarantee it."

"Ha! That's not a threat."

"It is when you mean it to mean what I mean it to mean."

"Meaning?"

"You're boaf talkin' junk," Groan rumbled, wrenching free from his bonds with one almighty flex. "Eever give us the ring or die."

Count Craven smiled, and motioned for his guards to shuffle back. "There is no ring," he said calmly. "And we're already dead." He rose from his throne and swept an indicating hand over the assembly. "By all means, try to fight us; you will fail. We have no blood to shed and all the time in the world in which to overcome you. Now, are you going to go quietly, or do we have to—"

"Master!"

The zombie captain entered the throne room from a side door and limped its way through the throng.

Count Craven turned a tired eye toward him. "Well?"

"Um . . . sorry to trouble you again, master, but what should we do with the dwarf's head?"

"You what?" Groan boomed, looking around the room and noticing, for the first time, that Gordo wasn't present. "What've you dun ta GORDO?"

"I thought I told you to drown him," Craven said.

The guard nodded. "You did, master."

"And you beheaded him instead?"

"No, master, we're getting ready to drown him. I just wanted to know what you wanted us to do with his head."

Craven's face was a terrible mask of confusion. "I don't understand," he said. "Isn't it on his shoulders?"

"One is, master," the captain confided. "The other's around his waist."

Craven raised one desiccated brow and turned his attention back to the warriors.

"You have a two-headed dwarf?" he inquired, with something approaching admiration.

"Not a two-headed dwarf," came a voice from outside, followed by a commotion. Gordo Goldeaxe appeared in the doorway, shouldered the last remaining zombies away from him, and held his head up high. "But a dwarf holding the head of your own nephew, Loogie Lambontroff!"

"Hello again, Uncle!" the head exclaimed.

There was a communal gasp, a series of shouts, and then the room erupted with violence.

"Kill them!" Craven screamed, retrieving a black staff from beside his throne and holding it aloft. "Kill them all!"

Groan bowled into the zombie carrying his sword, Gape wolf-whistled for his own two blades, and Gordo Goldeaxe did the first thing that came into his head. He threw it.

The zombie horde dived left and right as the screaming skull of Loogie Lambontroff somersaulted across the room. Not for the first time that day, it was beginning to get very angry indeed. . . .

FIFTEEN

IT WAS MIDNIGHT in Phlegm, and the keep was shrouded in darkness. Somewhere on the first floor, a wire carefully worked its way into a lock and forced a resounding click from the mechanism.

The door to Susti's bedchamber creaked open, and the princess stepped outside. The sentries on duty were fast asleep.

"Are you sure about this, ma'am?" Bronwyn panted. She'd had enough excitement for one day. For one lifetime, come to that.

"Shhh!" Susti warned. "Just get back inside and stay quiet. If you want to help, you can stuff my bed full of cushions."

She turned and tiptoed off along the corridor, clutching a candle dish in one hand and a mace in the other.

At the first T-junction, she slipped up behind the duty guard and clubbed him into unconsciousness. She decided not to bother dragging him into a nook; time was of the essence, and besides, he looked far too heavy for that.

Susti crept to the top of the outer dungeon stairwell and began to descend. On the ground floor, she had to stay low in order to avoid the corridor patrol, and came dangerously close to killing the keep's cat when it clawed at her as she crouched in the shadows.

Eventually, the patrol came and went, and the cat received its just deserts in the shape of some very hot wax.

Susti unhooked the latch of the dungeon door and stepped down into the glowing darkness.

Down.

Down.

Down.

Torchlight flared on the walls, and various nocturnally inclined prisoners began their midnight moaning sessions. Susti guessed that her father would be in the dankest, dirtiest cell in the dungeon, and headed toward it.

She was wrong.

Three half-naked ogres, a moon troll, two muggers, and a woman of the night later, she finally found the king in a cell not entirely unlike his own bedchamber. There were no guards on duty, and the key dangled from a convenient hook beside the door.

"F-father? Are you okay?" Susti called, reaching for the key. "Can you speak? Have they hurt you?"

King Phew rose from his prison bed. "No, my dear, I'm fine. Really, I am. What are you doing here?"

"I've come to get you out! I've come to rescue you!"

She turned the key in the lock and flung open the door, stepping back to indicate the empty corridor.

"C'mon, we're going to steal a cart or something. . . ."

The king sighed. "And where would we go? You heard Modeset; there isn't a kingdom in Illmoor that'd help me take my throne back from him!"

Susti nodded. "I agree with you, Father, but I *do* know some people who might—"

"Oh, really?" said a voice. Duke Modeset appeared at the doorway, flanked by General Crikey and an embarrassed-looking Pegrand. "Do tell."

Susti squinted to see into the shadows behind the general. There didn't seem to be any more guards outside in the corridor.

"I'm not telling you anything," she said, readying her mace. "And you haven't the brains to guess!"

Modeset rubbed his chin thoughtfully. "I haven't the brains to guess what?" he said. "That you're planning to flee the city and warn Groan Teethgrit and his rowdy mob about my plan, in a pathetic attempt to gain their allegiance?" He sighed and shook his head. "Two things, *Your Highness*: first, I doubt very much whether you'd make it past the more than fifty guards I've posted on the main gate, and second, according to a report from two of Phlegm's finest, the Teethgrits and Goldeaxe have already crossed the Washin, and will, by now, be having their insides removed by the zombie lord of Rintintetly. In fact, I have already sent a message to my fellow lords confirming it! Ha-ha-ha-ha!"

Susti's face fell, and she lowered her mace. "Of course," Modeset mimicked, "there's always your wild friend from the jungles. Oh . . . but what am I saying? My men drowned him in the river this evening. I'm so very sorry. Now, are you going to put down your weapon peacefully and return to your quarters, or are we going to have to do things the hard way?"

Susti glanced at her father's wretched expression, and reluctantly held out her mace for collection. Modeset grinned, Pegrand breathed a sigh of relief, and General Crikey strode over to retrieve the weapon.

Everything that happened next, happened in a blur of bewilderment and fury. . . .

It wasn't the first time Gordo Goldaxe had witnessed the emergence of a twinling; in fact, it wasn't even the first time *that* day. Still, the sight took his breath away. It was almost indescribable.

Put simply: he'd thrown a head that'd landed on its feet. That is, Loogie had simply sprouted another body, fully formed, *in midair*. The twinling, which'd started off as a red mist, was solid by the time it hit the ground. Cursing unnameable obscenities, it had promptly gone tearing up the hall like a thing possessed—which, of course, it *was*—reached the count before he could summon anything with his staff, and was currently trying to unscrew the zombie lord's decrepit skull. It was all very entertaining to watch, and, from a confrontational point of view, it had turned the tide of the battle.

Groan, ever the resourceful combatant, had quickly realized that his sword was redundant in their present situation, and had also figured out that the farther you threw a zombie, the longer it took the thing to stagger back.

Gape, usually by far the smarter of the two, was still persisting with his swords, and had several deep gashes in his chest as a result.

Gordo had leaped up onto the back of one of the larger zombies and was riding around on it, swinging his axe whenever the opportunity presented itself. He was also watching the Lambontroff versus Craven struggle with increasing curiosity.

Dark Loogie was winning. It'd pressed two thumbs into the eye sockets of its erstwhile uncle and was literally pushing the life right out of him.

"You stole my chicken!" it screamed. "You thieeef!"

There was a final, strangled scream, and the count collapsed into a crumpled heap. The move proved to be a domino effect, and, one by one, all of the count's minions succumbed to a similar fate, tumbling to the floor like unwanted rags.

Groan felt the zombie he was holding on to go limp, and tossed it aside.

Gape took two last swings at his own aggressors as they dropped, and Gordo landed on top of his makeshift horse with a cheer of victory.

"We did it!" he cried. "Can you believe that? Are we the toughest bunch of nutcases on the jetty or what?"

"I am," Groan bellowed. "You two didn't do nothin'. 'Sides, how we gonna find that ring now?"

"Hold your hors—" Gordo started, but Gape interrupted him.

"Not now, fellas. We've got trouble. . . ."

The three warriors looked up toward the throne, where Loogie Lambontroff's twinling was finishing off the count's staff. It raised the weapon high above its head and snapped it over one knee. Then it brandished both halves of the staff and came at them, screaming bloody murder. . . .

Stump awoke, freezing cold.

He was hungry, thirsty, and not a little annoyed. Still, he reflected, at least the guards had gone. He looked up at the full moon and tried to work out where he'd come ashore. It didn't take him long. . . .

He was on the eastern bank of the Washin, and the bordering trees of Rintintetly seemed to reach out toward him. He'd heard about the woods, of course. Everyone had. If the rumors were to be believed, they contained nothing but terrible danger and almost certain death. Then again, the same could be said for virtually any forest in Illmoor. Stump was at home in forests, woods, and jungles, but he usually liked to keep his base of operations in the southern stretches, like the Carafat, Helter Glades, or Shademost. This was new territory, and despite the come-hither wave of the trees, it didn't look too inviting.

Still, he had to get away somehow. It looked as though the duke was baying for his blood. He wondered about Phlegm's reach, guard-wise. Would it stretch up to Spittle, down to the Twelve? Hmm . . .

The best thing, he decided, would be to wait until morning and then go into Rintintetly. That way, he could follow the wood south and eventually emerge near the old Dullitch road.

First things first.

Stump looked around for a good-size rock, and went fishing in the moonlight.

Gape swung out his swords as the twinling rushed

toward him. He caught it with the first, missed with the second, and found himself hurtling backward across the hall, before he could even think about trying for a kick.

The twinling looked down at the cut that the warrior's sword had made in its arm, and grinned at the sight of its own blood.

Gordo was next up. He ran screaming at the creature, leaped into the air, and swung his battle-axe in a vertical arc. The twinling caught the weapon just below the blade, wrenching it away from the dwarf. Gordo rallied quickly, flinging himself to the ground and successfully sweeping the legs of the dark twin. It crashed to the floor, then spun around with such force that both its legs smashed into Gordo at the same time.

The dwarf shot across the flagstones like a flicked coin, disappearing through a window in a shower of glass.

The twinling cackled evilly, then raced across the room at Groan . . .

. . . who caught it in midair and snapped it like a twig.

There was a sudden eruption of flame, and the twinling vanished.

"Thank the gods for that," said the head of Loogie Lambontroff, looking up at Groan from amidst the smoking remains. "I thought we were in real trouble then."

"Help! Somebody help me!"

Gape staggered to his feet, and the two warriors hurried over to the window, pulling Gordo up from the ledge below with comparatively little effort.

"I'd say it's about time," Gordo spat, noticing that Groan had Loogie's head under one arm. "I see we're *ahead* of the game once again."

"Very funny," said Loogie miserably. "You know, I really should've grown back by now."

"I dun' care if you never grow back," Groan roared. "Tell us where the count keeps 'is chickens."

Loogie sniffed. "Don't know that I will."

"If you don't," said Gape, retrieving his swords, "I might start taking a dangerous interest in sport. I hear deathball is a lot of fun."

"All right, all right!" Loogie spluttered. "He keeps his chickens in a big coop in the gardens, but—"

"Good."

"Wait a min—"

"Shut it."

"Fine!"

Gape made an exaggerated gesture with his arm. "Lead on. . . ."

"Have it your way," the head muttered. "You'll need to go back through the door at the far end."

The group slowly began to head for the exit, but halfway across the floor, Gordo's sixth sense started tingling. It was a strange sensation, and one that seldom affected the dwarf unless he was about to miss out on something special.

"Stop!" he said suddenly.

Groan and Gape paused in the doorway and peered back at him.

"What is it?" the younger Teethgrit inquired, squinting at the dwarf. "You need a breather after your little trip through the window?"

Gordo shook his head. "There's something else in this room."

Groan stepped back through the door, and both brothers began to look around. After a few minutes, Gordo came to his senses and tapped Loogie on the top of his head.

"Yes?"

"Am I right?" asked the dwarf. "Is there something in this room that we're not seeing?"

The head sniffed. "Like what? Hidden treasure or something?"

"I dunno: you tell me."

"Hmm . . . I don't think so. There's a door you might be interested in, though—"

Gordo grinned. "I knew it," he said. "Where?"

"Behind the throne, but don't get excited; it doesn't contain the secret wealth of Illmoor or anything like that."

"Does it contain the secret wealth of Wemeru?"

The head twitched a few times, then sighed, "Scientifically speaking, *yes*."

"That'll do."

The warriors made for the steps that led to the throne, dashed up them two at a time and, together, heaved the giant chair to the flagstones.

Sure enough, there was a door in the wall behind it.

"Get it open!"

Groan's broadsword was the first to breach the gap between the door and the wall. Gape soon joined him, driving both swords in to give the team extra leverage. There was a hiss of escaping air, an audible creak, and the door scraped open.

"Look, why are you doing this?" Loogie complained. "I thought you wanted to find Lady Khan—"

"We do," said Gordo. "But if there's a gold deposit in there, then obviously we have to put that first."

He glanced at Groan and Gape for support, but both of them were looking doubtful.

"Look," Gape said, snatching a burning torch from a nearby wall bracket and peering beyond the door. "What *exactly* is up there?"

"I told you," Loogie muttered. "The scientific wealth of Wemeru."

"I don' wan' no si-an-tif-ic welf," Groan thundered. "I wan' welf you can buy stuff wiv."

"That door leads to the top of the pyramid," said the head. "And I'm warning you, it's one hell of a trek. If I were you I'd camp here and go up in the morning."

There was a vague murmur of agreement before Gordo conceded the point and slumped, exhausted, to the ground. Groan and Gape had a brief discussion about the best way to start a campfire and wandered off to collect a few zombies for kindling.

They slept peacefully, albeit in shifts.

Susti paused for a second to take stock of the situation. Somehow, she'd managed to knock General Crikey back with such force, he'd bowled into

Modeset and Pegrand, and now all three were rolling around in the corridor like stuck turtles.

She seized the opportunity, and, grabbing her father by the elbow, she rushed outside. She snatched a dagger from Crikey's belt, kicking him in the face before he could muster a reaction. Pegrand got similar treatment from King Phew, while Modeset had the common sense to stay down and wait for reinforcements. Unfortunately, the duke's luck wasn't in, and he felt a dagger prick his throat.

"Get up," Susti ordered, pressing the blade a little further. "You're a hostage."

Modeset struggled to his feet. "You'll never get away with this," he said, staying unnervingly calm as they shuffled back along the corridor. "I've got troops watching every wall in the city, and they'll have forty arrows in your back before you even get out of the keep. Ha-ha-ha!"

Susti smiled at the duke's laughter, and brought her mouth close to his ear. "We're not going to leave the city through the main gate," she whispered. "We're leaving through the network of tunnels that lead from the lower kitchens to the outer wall."

King Phew flashed a smile of his own. "That's the beauty of being overthrown in your own kingdom," he said. "You always know things the usurper doesn't know."

Crikey and Pegrand were both on their feet, and inching ever so slightly forward.

"I'm warning you," Susti cried out from the end of the corridor. "One more step, and I'll slit his gizzard."

"Really, my dear," King Phew complained. "That's not the sort of language I'd expect from a princess."

Susti sighed. "Considering the day I've had, Father, I think I'm being remarkably reserved. Now, do you think you could run ahead and clear the way?"

"Me?" The king looked doubtful. "How, for goodness' sake?"

"Grab a torch from the wall," Susti advised him.

He did as he was told.

"Good. Now, anyone who gets in your way, you can crack them over the head with it."

"I really don't know about this. . . ."

"Father, you're as bad as Bronwyn. Are you the King of Phlegm or not?"

"Well, yes—"

"Then bloody well get out there and prove it!"

SIXTEEN

IT WAS VERY EARLY morning in Wemeru, and Gordo, Groan, and Gape had been ascending the pyramid for more than an hour. The steps were covered in cobwebs, and strange hieroglyphics adorned the walls.

"How much longer?" Gape complained.

Gordo waved a hand. "Quiet!"

"This is a waste of ti—"

"Shh! I can see a door."

"Well, whoop-de-do!" Gape mimicked. "Gordo's found himself another door. Let's have a party, shall we?"

Groan said nothing, but a heavy sigh betrayed his opinion.

Gordo had hurried up to the door and was already using his axe to prize it open. By the time

Gape and Groan reached the top of the stairs, the dwarf had already slipped through the door and into the chamber beyond. The brothers reluctantly followed.

Three enormous coffins dominated the wide, drafty room at the top of the pyramid, and each of these was wired to a series of squat and bizarrely shaped mechanical machines. The room looked part laboratory, part mausoleum.

Gordo sneezed as he inadvertently breathed in some dust.

"What the—"

"It's a translocator," the head explained, closing its eyes as Gordo's nasal discharge engulfed him.

"A what?"

"A star mechanism: an earth shifter."

"I've never seen anything like it in my life," Gape said, staring around him with bewildered awe.

"Yeah, well, we've always built magikanic machines. In fact, we were practicing technomancy before the rest of Illmoor was walking upright."

Groan's face was a network of creases. He hadn't understood anything anyone had said since he'd entered the room. It felt as though he were walking among foreigners.

"So how do you use it?" Gape managed, still aghast.

The head puffed out a long sigh. "Well," it said. "Basically, it uses stockpiled energy to realign the stars, only it doesn't really do that. In actual fact, it realigns Illmoor."

"What's real-ine mean?" asked Groan irritably.

Gordo shrugged. "I think it's a fancy way of saying 'to move things.'"

"Oh," Gape said, sounding disappointed. "Nothing special, then."

"I think it's pretty incredible, actually," said Loogie defensively. "If I'd found out I could travel anywhere in Illmoor simply by sticking a metal rod on a map and climbing into a coffin with a collar round my neck, I'd be well amazed. Still, that's people for you, isn't it? I suppose nothing impresses barbarians."

The head finished its incessant chatter and looked up. Groan and Gape were both staring at it with incredulous expressions.

"Do you want to go through that again, *slowly*?" said Gordo slowly.

"It's just one straight tunnel," General Crikey said,

pointing to the map he'd laid out on the keep's rarely used war table. He hadn't had a wink of sleep all night, and was eager to retrieve the troublesome princess as soon as possible. "We could send soldiers in at either end; cut them off. We can easily reach the outer entrance before they can."

"No," said Pegrand, shaking his head. "We can't risk any harm to the duke."

Crikey rolled his tired eyes. He still couldn't quite work out why he was taking orders from the duke's manservant, but then, it *had* been a strange night.

"Then what, may I ask, do *you* suggest?"

Pegrand thought for a moment before replying. Then he rubbed his tired eyes, sucked in some air, and laid both hands flat on the map.

"Well," he began, pursing his lips for effect, "we could go in at either end, cut them off."

Crikey rolled his eyes. "But that's what I just said!"

"Yes, but I meant just you, me, and a couple of guards."

"Fine."

Crikey strode across to the room's giant gong and sounded a deafening tone. After a few minutes, the two guards who'd trailed Stump to the river the previous day, came sauntering through the door.

Pegrand frowned at them. "Are you the only soldiers in the city, or something?"

They shrugged.

"We're the only two not guarding the wall," said one.

"Does it matter?" Crikey protested. "You wanted a couple of guards; here they are."

Pegrand nodded. "Very good," he said. "Now, I want you three to wait at this end of the tunnel. I'll go in from the outer wall end and drive them back toward you."

Crikey looked confused. "Us three," he said. "You mean you're going into the tunnel alone?"

"Oh, no," Pegrand said, shaking his head. "I'm going in with the duke's dog."

There was a sudden outbreak of muffled laughter.

"You can't be serious," Crikey said, a twisted smile on his face. "You're putting three fully armed men at *this* end of the tunnel as a blockade—"

"That's right."

"And *you* expect to be able to drive the princess and her father back toward *us*?"

"Got it in one."

"The princess has a dagger, and the king's probably picked up all manner of knives in the lower kitchen. You genuinely believe they'll run from a dog?"

"Oh, yes," said Pegrand. "They'll run, all right."

"Are you out of your *mind*?" Gape exclaimed. "This thing looks like it hasn't been used in a hundred years!"

"It's probably been a bit more than that," Loogie suggested. "Most of Craven's subjects thought it was a bit arcane."

Gordo shrugged, then turned to his companions and angrily threw down his axe. "Look," he snapped. "Do you two want to win the damn princess or not?"

There was an awkward silence.

"Well?"

"Yes."

"I s'pose."

"Then what are we waiting for? If we can get this whatsitcalled working, we can jump in and transport ourselves!"

"Where to?"

"To Kazbrack," the dwarf screamed. "To Fastrush Pass, to Windlass Eyrie!"

There was a vague murmur of agreement.

"It's probably still in working order," said Loogie encouragingly. "But if you ask me—"

"Just tell us how it works!"

"I did!"

Gordo wrenched the head from his belt and stared it in the eye.

"*Specifically*."

"Ah, right. I see what you mean. Turn me 'round, and I'll have a look."

Gordo twisted the head, gripping a tuft of hair between his thumb and forefinger.

"Right," said Loogie, when the room had stopped spinning. "Now listen carefully, because I'm working from memory, here. Okay, you see the big map of Illmoor on the far wall?"

Gape raised his torch, and the map appeared.

"That's the one; there should be three iron pointers attached to it. You need to place those on the different places you want to go."

Gordo put the head on a nearby bench, then wandered over to the map, climbed onto a dust-covered chair, and began to rearrange the markers.

"Good going," Loogie said. "Now, you should find three iron collars in the chest over by the wall.

You put those on before you climb into the coffins. They'll bring you back after exactly one hour. The levers you need to pull to get the whole thing started are just inside the lids. Got it?"

Gordo nodded. "Loud and clear," he said, turning to the Teethgrit brothers. "How about you two?"

"Yes," said Gape.

Groan nodded. "I ain't as stoopid as you fink," he rumbled.

"I'll see you both in Kazbrack, then," said Gape, locking his torch onto the wall bracket beside the map.

"Wait a minute. . . ."

"What?"

Gape scratched a hairy eyebrow. "Shouldn't we get the chicken's ring, first?"

Gordo looked back toward the longest staircase in Illmoor.

"After you," he said.

"Fine," said Gape. "We'll get it later. I just thought I'd mention it, that's all."

Gordo handed out the collars, and the three of them climbed wearily into the coffins, pulling the lids closed behind them.

There was a series of clicks, then silence. After a

time, a dull and monotonous hum began to resound in the room. The machines beside each coffin pulsated with ancient energy. Suddenly, the chamber (and, unbeknownst to Loogie, the entire pyramid) was flooded with light.

Then, just as swiftly, it was gone, leaving the small chamber bathed in flickering torchlight.

The new silence was pierced by a loud creak, and the lid to Gordo's coffin swung open.

The dwarf stuck out his head. "Am I in Kazbrack?"

"If you are, it's very similar to Wemeru," said Loogie gloomily.

"Damn it!" Gordo barked, as Groan and Gape emerged from their individual coffins. "Does anything in this place work?"

"Hey, it was *your* idea," said the head. "If it's any consolation, you put all the markers in different places."

Gordo shrugged, unlocking his collar and throwing it to the floor.

"So?"

"So, the three of you would have gone to three separate places!"

"And you didn't think to tell us that before we climbed in?"

"I couldn't see the map, with your fat head in the way!"

"Will you two stop whining at each other?" Gape said, casting off his own collar and heading for the door. "The whole thing was a stupid idea anyway. As far as I'm concerned, there are two ways to go somewhere: by horse or by foot. Now, are we going to argue all day, or are we going to find this chicken?"

"Oi," Groan called from across the room. "Why can't I get this damn collar off me neck?"

Zombie chickens, the party discovered, were pretty much like ordinary chickens. The only difference being, they pecked less.

Groan clambered over the barrier and wandered among the fowl, kicking several out of the way as he progressed toward the henhouse that Loogie had indicated. He was in a very bad mood; nobody had been able to prize the collar from his neck, and now it looked, to all intents and purposes, as if he were stuck with it.

"A little way to your left!" Loogie was shouting. "That's it! One of the compartments should have a crown above it."

Gape and Gordo hurried after the giant barbarian, arriving at the correct cubbyhole just as Groan spotted it.

Sure enough, there was a chicken squawking inside, and right as mustard, it had a tiny crown on its head. The henhouse looked old, but paled in comparison to the chicken. Even Count Craven had looked young compared to the chicken.

Loogie almost wept when he saw the creature, and was positively distraught when Groan—having turned the chicken upside down a few times—jammed a finger up its behind.

"What're you doing!" the head exclaimed.

"Checkin' for rings," Groan muttered. He rooted around for a while, then let the good lady fall to the grass. She peered up at them, bleary-eyed, then strutted toward the shadowy end of the coop.

"No ring, eh?" Gape ventured, studying Groan's blank expression just in case his brother had palmed it. "Maybe it's hidden in—"

"There is no ring." Groan and Gape both turned to consider Gordo, who reached for Loogie's head and rested it on his forearm.

"Are you listening to that *thing* again?" Gape ventured, indicating the head with his thumb. "Because I for one am getting sick and tired of—"

"Shut up."

"Listen—"

"You 'eard 'im."

Gape stared at Groan's serious expression and was about to laugh, when he thought better of it.

"Supposing there really is no *ring*," Gordo suggested, staring up at them both with a worried brow.

"At last, some sense!" said the head of Loogie. "That's what I've been trying to tell you for the last three hours!"

"Go on," said Gape dubiously.

Gordo shrugged and peered down at his cranial companion. "Remember when you were telling us about your days in Dullitch, and what an expert you were in legendary lost treasures?"

"Yes. I'm glad you were listen—"

"Well, what are you like on geography?"

Loogie grinned. "Superb. I've got three dip—"

"We're not interested in your qualifications, Loogie," Gordo reasoned. "We're interested in your *knowledge*."

The head tried to nod. "No problem," it said. "Fire away!"

Gordo glanced from the head, to Groan, and back again. "Have you ever heard of a place called Windlass Eyrie?" he asked.

"'Course."

"Kazbrack?"

"Naturally."

"Fastrush Pass?"

"Hmm . . . yes, yes I have."

"Well"—Gordo suddenly gritted his teeth—"WHY THE BLOODY HELL DIDN'T YOU SAY SOMETHING EARLIER?"

"I told you I had six medals fro—"

"You didn't tell us you knew about all the spittin' quest locations!"

"You didn't ask!"

"Didn't ask?" Gordo boggled at him. "You do realize that if the coffin machine had worked, we'd have been halfway across the continent by now!"

"Yeah," Groan added. "An' I wouldn' 'ave a choker wrapped 'round me neck."

Loogie sniffed. "I'm sorry," he said. "Maybe I was a bit resentful. I mean, after all, you *did* cut my head off. That sort of thing can really make you *biased*."

Gordo rolled his eyes. "Are you going to tell us something useful or not?"

Loogie sucked in his bottom lip. "Which one do you want to know about first?"

"Windlass Eyrie."

"Hmm, that's watched—"

"Twenty-four hours a day by the harpies of Narrow Death Rise, yes, we know that, but have you ever heard of a legendary treasure chest being buried up there?"

Loogie thought for a moment.

"Definitely not," he said. "In fact, I'm fairly sure that there's no record of a treasure chest being buried anywhere in the Finion Mountains. If there is, it's one the society didn't know about—I spent six months filing all their maps for them. It's certainly not a *legendary* treasure."

"What about the Idol of Needs?" Gape demanded.

The head tried to nod, and almost toppled. "Now, that *does* exist," it said. "Of course, it turned out to be just a flask full of water: a bit of an irony, considering that water is really all you "needs" to survive. Ha-ha-ha! Anyway, it was found by the society during the later part of the Dual Age and taken to Legrash. I think it's in a glass case or something."

Groan's giant brows knitted together.

"So it's definitely not in Kazbrack, then?" Gordo prompted.

"Kazbrack?" the head exclaimed. "Good gods, no. There's nothing in Kazbrack except hordes of great big bloodthirsty demons. That island's an absolute hellhole, the sort of place you send people if you don't want them to come back."

"What 'bout the dragon?" Groan boomed. "That livin'?"

Gordo explained the legend of Torche to Loogie Lambontroff.

The head pursed its lips. "Hmm . . . never having heard much about Fastrush Pass, I couldn't say for sure," it admitted. "But I'd be pretty surprised if any dragon turned out to have jeweled eyes. How would it see, for goodness' sake?"

Gordo nodded, took two deep breaths, and looked around at Groan and Gape.

"Well, I don't know about you," he said. "But I'm very, very angry."

SEVENTEEN

KING PHEW progressed along the low tunnel, his head slightly bowed and his torch thrust out in front of him. Susti brought up the rear, her knife still pressed firmly against Modeset's throat.

"How much longer?" she moaned, trying to peer over the duke's shoulder at the receding shape of her father.

"A few more twists and turns," the king admitted. "These passages can be a maze, my darling."

"You're making a big mistake, Phew," said Modeset, grimacing as the knife edge dug in. "As soon as the other rulers find out—"

"Yes, I've been thinking about that," said the king reflectively. "And I'm not sure they *would* take your side, considering that most of them hate and despise you. I know that Curfew's your cousin, but didn't you execute his mother before all that business with the virgin sacrifices? He can't have forgotten that, surely?"

Modeset didn't say anything, but the king could hear him muttering under his breath.

"Father, I—"

"Shhh!" King Phew came to an abrupt stop, then turned to face Susti and put a finger to his lips. "There's someone coming! Go back!"

"We can't go back!" the princess protested. "The guards will be waiting for us at that end!"

King Phew sighed. "They'll be waiting for us at both ends," he said. "Crikey's probably found the underground maps."

"Jolly good," Modeset muttered, wincing when Susti slapped him on the side of his head.

"We might as well turn back," the king continued, his shoulders sagging.

"Yes, I would if I were you," the duke urged. "You really don't stand a chance."

"Maybe we can convince the guards to return their allegiance to us?"

Modeset laughed. "I wouldn't bank on it," he said. "Your soldiers are particularly stupid, even by Dullitch standards. You should educate them once in a while; does wonders for allegiance, an education."

The noise from the end of the passage was growing louder. It sounded like two different sets of footsteps: one evenly paced and the other . . .

"Dogs!" the king exclaimed. "I think they've got dogs with them."

"Our guards don't *have* dogs," said Susti doubtfully. "Maybe it's just an echo thrown up by people breathing."

"No." Modeset smiled. "I think you'll find that's most definitely a dog, Your Highness."

"She wouldn' o' lied," Groan boomed, shoving Gape aside as he stomped from the great pyramid into the hollow streets of Wemeru. "She's 'n love wiv me."

"Actually, I think she preferred *me*," Gape muttered, ignoring the dwarf's blatant glare. "But speaking objectively, *big brother*, I think we've BOTH been done."

Groan rounded on him. "What? Just o' cause some mangy ol' 'ead sez so?"

"Hey, who're you calling mang—"

Gordo was quick to stifle Loogie's question, but

Gape was staring at Groan with a false smile playing on his lips.

"Are you *really* so stupid that you'd rather go in search of a treasure that doesn't exist than *admit* you've been taken for a fool by a woman?"

"Both of you have," Gordo observed, adding, "and don't look at me: I'm just the backup."

Groan sniffed. "I reckon we shoul' go ta Kazbrack, get the idol an'—"

"For the love of MERCY! There *is no idol*."

"Yeah, so '*e* sez." Groan thumbed at the head. "You'd 'ave to be a real dillo ta take 'is 'dvice."

Gape rolled his eyes. "You'd have to be a real dillo NOT to. He knows about history and geography. Do we? Do we hel—"

"We could go," said Gordo. He'd spoken the words quietly, but now everyone was staring at him, apart from Loogie (who was staring—not by choice—at the dwarf's groin). "You know; just to make sure."

"WHAT?" said Gape incredulously. "You can't be serious!"

"Well, Kazbrack is really close now. We could just nip—"

"You want to go across another expanse of water, to an island infested with demons, *just to make sure* there isn't an idol there? You do realize that makes you totally insane?"

"Yeah, but if we fin' one, I reckon' it might make me a prince," Groan said, beaming.

"And if you don't?" said Loogie, slightly annoyed that he'd been rotated *away* from the conversation.

"If we don't," Gordo muttered, "we go back to Phlegm with a vengeance. Princess or no princess."

Gape shook his head and slumped onto the ground, staring down the main street of Wemeru with an angry glint in his eye.

Gordo lifted Loogie's head toward him. "I don't suppose the marvelous inventors of the incredible translocator ever got 'round to sea travel, did they?"

Loogie pursed his lips. "Afraid not," he said. "I don't think they really liked the ocean."

Gordo shared a look with Groan and Gape, then made to fasten the head back onto his belt.

"Mind you," Loogie went on, "there's always the pedal sky-spinner, but they never properly tested th—what? What're you all lookin' at?"

Pegrand Marshall appeared in the tunnel. From what Susti could determine, he was attempting, unsuccessfully, to hold back a *blur* on a lead.

King Phew stepped back and swallowed. The dog didn't just look mad; it looked positively *deranged*.

Pegrand grimaced in the glowering shadows. "You have a five-minute head start," he said, snatching a torch from the wall. "And then I'm going to let him go."

Susti peered over Modeset's shoulder at her father, who was frozen to the spot with fear.

"Er, I'd make the most of it if I were you," Pegrand urged them. "I don't think I can hold him much longer.

Susti turned to run, tripped on a loose stone, and fell down, holding the knife above her like a shield.

King Phew tried to make his feet move, but they were rooted. He gave a little whimper instead.

"That's it; I can't—"

Pegrand gave a gasp of pain, then let go of the lead and watched in horror as the dog scampered forward.

Time seemed to stop as Vicious flew through the air . . .

. . . dashed between King Phew's trembling legs . . .

. . . and went straight for Modeset's throat. It missed and fastened its jaws onto the duke's arm instead.

Susti elbowed her way back through the tunnel as the duke lurched from wall to wall, his fingers locked around the dog's snapping maw.

"I'm sorry, milord," Pegrand called. "I really thought it'd go for the others."

"Argghh!" Modeset cried. "You should've known better, damn it! This dog is the most unpredic-taaaaahhh!"

He stumbled a few feet and, with one final burst of strength, prized the dog's jaws off his arm and lobbed it down the corridor. It landed on its feet, spun around, and set its sights on Pegrand, a low growl birthing in its throat.

"Er, b-bad boy," the manservant started. "*Naughty* boy. STAY!"

By the time Vicious leaped, Pegrand had already turned and bolted up the corridor like a man possessed. The dog quickly gave chase.

King Phew let out a heavy sigh of relief. His daughter, who'd managed to struggle back onto her feet, had already realigned her knife with the duke's throat.

"That won't be necessary," said a voice, and the princess felt a crossbow bolt in the small of her back. "Let's have that blade, Your Highness."

General Crikey's sly grin appeared in the semi-darkness like some freakish phantom. There were two more smiles behind him.

Modeset stepped away from the princess and grinned. "You've made a valiant attempt to escape, Susti," he said, rubbing his wounded arm. "But it's over. Now, I'll say it one last time: you can either come along quietly, or you can die. The choice is yours entirely."

Susti took one last regretful look at her father, and tossed the knife to General Crikey, who caught it and tucked it into his belt.

"Now, listen up," he instructed as the duke squeezed past him. "Everyone follow me . . . and no stragglers."

Groan, Gordo, and Gape had been directed by Loogie to the top of a step pyramid on the east side of Wemeru, where they had located the city's apparently "notorious" sky-spinner.

The contraption squatted on the flat roof of the pyramid. It was an ugly machine, with five seats fixed below four giant wooden blades. Beneath each seat was an ancient-looking set of pedals. The whole thing looked antiquated.

Gordo waddled around the sky-spinner a few times before coming to a conclusion.

"It'll never fly," he muttered. "Not in a million years."

"Of course it'll *fly*," Loogie assured him. "It's *enchanted*."

Gape grinned. "What, like the translocator?"

"*That* was different. I've actually *seen* this working. Er . . . well, *almost* working. We're two men short, but the controls are basically—"

"Can I guess?" Gordo interrupted.

"Erm . . . go ahead."

"Do we, by any chance, start pedaling frantically until it takes off?"

"Yes! Simple, isn't it?"

Gape looked doubtful. "Don't we need a runway of some kind?"

"Well," said the head. "That's what the pyramid's for, you see."

Every head swiveled to regard Loogie.

"You don't mean . . ." Gape began.

"Yeah, that's right. We drive off the edge of the

pyramid, pedal fiercely, and hope we're aloft by the time we get below the tree line."

There was an awkward silence.

"You know what I think?" Gordo hazarded. "I think that bloke with the shoe-sole boat'd fit right in here."

EIGHTEEN

"RIGHT. On the count of three: one-two-three-RUN! That's it, pick up your feet, we're near the edgeaaarrgghghgghh! Pedal! Pedal, damn it! Faster! Faster! Faster! Faster! FFAASSTTEERR!"

"I can't pedal; my leg's stuck!"

"We're all gonna die!"

"Groan! Take over Gape's pedals!"

"I can't; I'm doin' me own."

"Loogie—"

"What am *I* supposed to pedal with? My teeth?"

"Argghghgh! Now my leg's stuck."

"How come *nothing* these people make works properly?"

"We're gonna hit the trees, we're gonna hit the damn trees!"

"Pedal, then! Peddddaaalll!"

"My pedal's come off! Oh, no it hasn't—it's just slipped down a bit—"

"Our lords who aren't in Illmoor, cursed be thy name. Hallowed be the sound of them burning underground. . . ."

"I love you, Groan."

"Shut up and pedal, you bloody midget!"

"Don't you call me a midget, Gape Tearghh! I don't believe it! We're flying—we're flying!"

Groan and Gape paid him no attention. They were both staring, openmouthed at the far horizon. The sky-spinner had cleared the treetops and was beginning to rise high over Rintintetly, carried on a wind that seemed to have come from nowhere.

"I told you," said Loogie's muffled voice, from the seat next to Gordo. In all the excitement, he'd accidentally rolled onto his face. "Pure enchantment, that is. One hundred percent pure—"

"—sweat," finished Gape. "And a decent wind; otherwise, we'd all be pancakes."

"Yeah," Groan managed, his feet working the pedals so fast they literally hummed. "Damn zombie junk."

Loogie gave an exaggerated sigh. "Hey, don't knock it, pal," he muttered. "You're flying, aren't you?"

They were now some way above the forest roof, and the Nasbeck Ocean was fast approaching. Gape chanced a glance over one shoulder and saw that the pyramids of Wemeru were already fading dots in the distance.

Gape peered around at Groan. "Can you see it?" he asked.

"Eh?"

"Can you see the island?"

"Nah. Wha' 'bout you?"

"No, not yet."

"Hold me up!" Loogie protested. "I've got fantastic eyesight."

Gordo snatched up the head and passed it to Gape. "What if you drop him?"

"I won't."

"He'd better not; I don't fancy bouncin' *that* high."

The barbarian gripped Loogie tightly by the hair and held him aloft.

"See anything?"

"That would be tough, meathead. You've turned me the wrong way. All I can see is forest."

Gape sighed, then twisted his grip.

"Careful! Don't get me too close to the propellers! I nearly lost my nose, then!"

Gordo rolled his eyes. "Stop whining and *look*, damn it!"

"Okay, okay! Yeah, I can see something—a dot, but it's getting bigger."

There was a lengthy pause.

"Well?" Gape prompted. "C'mon, my arm's getting tired. I thought *he* said this thing was magical!"

"It is!" Loogie protested. "It's a tree that flies; what more do you want?"

"I want a break. . . ."

"Just keep going!" Loogie snapped. "The island's straight ahead. It looks like Kazbrack to me; there's a volcano on it."

"Great," Gordo muttered as Gape handed the head back to him. "We'll aim for that, then. Shall we?"

"'Ere," boomed Groan. "How d' we turn this fing?"

A look of concern crossed Loogie's features.

"I—"

"Never mind that," Gordo snapped. "How do we *land* it?"

The head grinned and said sheepishly: "I think you just stop pedaling. . . ."

* * *

"We haven't used this place for years," General Crikey muttered, staring up at the three figures chained to the wall. "It used to be the hall of records, now it doubles up as a handy holding pen for, how shall we say, *distinguished guests*."

Modeset smiled contentedly. "It should suffice."

"Why am I up here, ma'am?" Bronwyn called across to Susti, who occupied a set of manacles on the opposite wall.

"You're up there because you helped her to *deceive* us," said Crikey. "By stuffing the princess's bed with cushions, you made yourself a coconspirator. That's how treachery works, isn't it, lordship?"

Modeset nodded. "Exactly, General," he said. "Though I think Pegrand should probably join them up there for releasing my own dog against me."

"How is he?" Crikey asked, mock concern showing on his face.

"He'll live," Modeset assured him. "He was picked up by several of your *finest* at the main gate: superficial injuries."

"Did they find the dog?"

"Unfortunately, yes. The *creature* is back in its cage."

"Very good, lordship. The city is also secure, as

per your instructions. No one can get in *or* out, and we've got guards all over the wall."

"Superb, General: you've more than earned your stripes."

Crikey bowed low and departed, leaving Modeset alone with his prisoners.

"Excellent," the duke muttered. "A place for everyone, and everyone in their place. Now, people, let's get some well-deserved rest, shall we?"

The fire demons of Kazbrack were a devoutly religious community of creatures that kept themselves to themselves and never ventured beyond the boarders of their own tiny island. They worshipped Incendous, the god of flames, who lived on Kazbrack in the form of a great volcano. Incendous was not a greedy god, but he did demand sacrifices on an irregular basis and—if these weren't provided with swift abandon—he would literally blow his top. However, Incendous was not unkind: he slept peacefully much of the time, and when he did require a sacrifice or two, he always ensured that the ocean would provide them. This could take a number of days, but Incendous usually gave the demons plenty of time to prepare.

Today, however, Incendous was working in mysterious ways. Not only had he been grumbling steadily louder all morning, he had also decided to *fly* his sacrifices in on some sort of airborne workbench. Incendous, it seemed, was ravenous.

The demons were so overjoyed, they'd all gathered on the beach, determined to celebrate the arrival of the sacrifices in grand style.

The sacrifices themselves were not so keen to land.

"What're all those red spots on the beach?" said Gordo, squinting.

"They're fire demons," Loogie pointed out conversationally. "Creatures whose tattered skin is cursed to burn for all eternity."

"Whatever they are, they're dancing," said Gape.

"Can you imagine that?" Loogie went on. "Seriously, can you imagine having twenty-four-hour-a-day sunstroke for the rest of your life? It's no wonder they're all a bunch of psychopathic lunatics who slaughter anyone unfortunate enough to land on their island. Oh, and did you know they can actually transform themselves into living—"

"Whose idea was this again?" Gape said, staring pointedly at Gordo. "I know, we'll just land on the beach, pop along to the chief, ask him if he knows where we can find the Idol of Needs, and then hop back onboard our sky-spinner and drift away. What do you think?"

Gordo ignored him. Instead, the dwarf was gazing down at the beach with apparent horror.

"Keep pedaling," he muttered to Groan. "We're not going to land."

"Eh?"

"I said, 'we're not going to land.' Look at those things down there; they're all alight! It's not worth the risk. . . ."

"Wha' 'bout the idol?"

"There is no idol, Groan. We've been done."

"Great!" Gape screamed, working his legs a lot faster than he'd managed over Rintintetly. "You couldn't have decided that before we set out on this thing?"

Gordo shrugged. "I needed a while to think about it!"

"Told you so," muttered Loogie.

"Do me a favor," Gape snarled. "The next time you *need a while* to think about something, can you just say so? That way, we might actually get to keep some of our limbs. . . ."

"Wha' 'bout the princess?" Groan grumbled. "She wouldn' o' lied. . . ."

"Well, she *did*," said Gordo.

To the dwarf's surprise, Groan shrugged. "I fink I've gone off her 'nyway. . . ."

Gape coughed loudly. "Do you mind if we concentrate on the more immediate problems," he said. "Like what we're going to do about the ISLAND OF FIRE DEMONS RIGHT BELOW US AT THIS VERY SECOND?"

"Just keep pedaling!" Gordo shouted back. "We're going to go *around* the volcano."

"We'll never make it!" Gape moaned. "My legs are tired."

Gordo shook his head. "You've just got to fight through it! Look at Groan, he's been pedaling for ages, an' he's fine. . . ."

"No I ain't; 'sides, I fort we dint know 'ow to turn 'round?"

"We don't," Gordo said. "But I reckon all we have to do is lean the way we want to go. You know, all of us lean together, at the same time."

The demons of Kazbrack hadn't expected the sacrifice-delivery machine to go flying over their heads, but they reacted swiftly anyway. Within seconds, a hail of burning arrows exploded from the beach.

The sky-spinner rose and fell on the wind, which was doing its bit to put out most of the arrows before they reached the contraption.

"That last one nearly hit us," Gape observed, pedaling through the pain barrier as the great volcano loomed toward them through the wispy clouds.

"I know, I know!" said Gordo. He peered sideways at Groan, who was still sulking over the princess situation.

The sky-spinner was drawing level with the volcano. Gape looked down and saw that the demonic natives were in pursuit, dashing up the winding path that led to the top of the mountain. Some of the less intelligent ones were still shooting at them, but the sky-spinner was way out of reach.

Then something unexpected happened.

Firstly, a series of low and heavy rumbles echoed through the volcano. Secondly, the natives stopped dead in their tracks and dropped to their knees in prayer.

"What's happening?" Gape asked, staring at Gordo as if the dwarf constituted the standard repository of island wisdom.

Gordo shrugged. "How the hell should I know?" he snapped. "Now, on the count of three, I want everyone to lean *right*. Ready? One. Two. Th—"

There was an enormous, gargantuan explosion, and a cloud of dust and hot ash spewed from the top of the volcano.

"LEAN LEFT! LEAN LEFT! LEAN L-E-E-EFFFT!" Gordo screamed. The two barbarians quickly changed direction and followed his instructions, veering away from the volcano as a second wave of smaller explosions rocked the island.

Miraculously, the sky-spinner began to turn.

"It's working! It's working!" shouted Loogie, who, somewhat alarmingly, sounded surprised.

"KEEP PEDALING!" Gordo shouted at the two brothers, trying to keep his own pedals turning. He suddenly realized how lucky they had been to escape the first blast of ash, and quickly determined not to think about it until they were well clear of the island.

After ten minutes of incredible effort, the sky-spinner was realigned. Gape noticed that, as they zoomed back over the beach, there was no sign of the demons. Evidently, they now had more important things to do than pursue intruders. The warrior smiled with relief and returned his attention to Gordo.

"Loogie," the dwarf was saying, "Loogie . . . ?"

"Hello? Yes?"

"H-how many people does it take to fly this thing, do you think?"

The head twitched its nose. "Er . . . well, three, *obviously*."

Gordo sighed. "Do you think we could do it with two, in shifts? Otherwise, I don't think we'll get over the ocean."

"Good idea," Gape said, panting heavily, "but I'm taking the first break. . . ."

He was about to stop pedaling, when Gordo suddenly let out a long breath, his shoulders sagging.

"I'm sorry," he muttered. "I can't go on." He slowly stopped pedaling, then reached down and began to massage his throbbing legs.

Gape was the second to stray, and when his legs finally went, the sky-spinner dipped sharply. Groan did his level best to keep the machine in the air, but he was effectively doing the work of five people and, after more than an hour in the air, even the mighty barbarian wasn't quite up to that.

"We're finished," Loogie shouted. "We're going

right into the ocean! Somebody take hold of me, quick, before I drown!"

The situation looked bleak as the sky-spinner dived once more. It skimmed the top of the water a few times and looked to all intents and purposes as if it would end up dishing between the waves. Then, as if by magic, Groan found his second wind.

It took Gape and Gordo a few minutes to realize that they were still airborne, and Loogie—whose vantage point depended on which way he rocked—had to be told the good news.

Groan's hulking legs were pumping again with renewed vigor. The sky-spinner was beginning to climb. Relieved by their break and spurred on by Groan's dramatic show of endurance, Gordo and Gape began driving their own pedals.

And still, the sky-spinner climbed.

"Right," Gordo said, after a time. "Groan! Take a break."

The big barbarian didn't need to be told twice. He relaxed, but even though the sky-spinner dropped slightly, the others managed to keep it going. This went on for five minutes or more, after which, Groan took over and Gape had a break. It wasn't an ideal system, but it got the team over the

Nasbeck Ocean, and almost saw them safely to the banks of the Washin.

Then, on the western fringe of Rintintetly, something entirely unexpected happened.

"Ahh!"

A ring of fire had appeared around Gordo's throat, and it took the others a few seconds to realize that it was an arm.

The dwarf stopped pedaling immediately and reached for his battle-axe, screaming as the flaming appendage engulfed him. The fire demon appeared, grinning, behind him, its eyes literally burning into the top of Gordo's helmet.

"H-help m-me!"

Gape made to move, but Groan reached out an arm and forced him back.

Drawing his own broadsword, the giant barbarian wriggled out of his seat and tried to slash at the thing. The sky-spinner dipped considerably, and Gape gasped with effort as he tried to keep it airborne.

Groan had abandoned his sword attack and was attempting to beat the demon off using his fists. He succeeded only in scorching both hands.

Gordo, meanwhile, was experiencing the deadly

combination of being choked and burned at the same time.

"I was trying to tell you earlier," Loogie called helpfully. "They can turn into living flame."

"Great gods!" Gape exclaimed. "They weren't firing arrows; they were firing each *other*!"

"Only one of them hit us," the head went on. "Listen, you can't fight this thing! We need to get out now! All of us! We're low enough—look! All we need to do is leap out—the sky-spinner will land in the Washin!"

Gape gritted his teeth. "So?" he puffed.

"So, the water 'll kill it!"

"How come you know all this stuff?"

"It's just common sense! Now, come on!"

Gordo was the first to take the head's advice. He managed to slip under the demon's throat-lock, sustaining several burns in the process. Then he threw himself forward, making a frantic grab for Loogie on the way down, and plunged headfirst into the trees, the head tumbling after him.

Gape slipped out of his seat, and felt a sharp pain as the fire demon leaped onto his shoulder and sank its teeth deep into his neck.

Groan reached out and snatched the beast by its

fiery arm, burning himself badly in the process. He used all his strength to drive the creature away from his brother. Then he swiftly followed Gordo over the side of the sky-spinner before it could snatch hold of *him*.

Groan was hitting the first branches of the tallest trees just as Gape somersaulted after him. The three warriors crashed, crunched, and snapped their way downward.

Groan landed in a mercifully thick bush, while Gordo yelped in the nettle patch that'd broken his fall. Gape had swung a hundred and eighty degrees on a tree branch, and landed, inexplicably, on his feet, clutching at the burning wound on his neck.

There was a swift and very distant splash.

Loogie, who'd had his eyes closed throughout the fall, found himself snagged on the twig end of a thin and spindly branch. He was suspended by his left nose hole, and he was in intense pain.

"Can somebody get me down from here?" he inquired. "After all, I did get us out of a tight spot back there, and wherever you guys landed, we *are* very near the Washin. That's good, isn't it? Hello? Anyone?"

NINETEEN

THE INNKEEPER of the Welcroft Inn had spent most of the morning fixing his door. Not usually a man who prided himself on DIY, he was, nevertheless, considerably proud of his handiwork.

So was his wife.

"It's as good as new!" she said, with an expanding smile.

The innkeeper beamed.

"Aye. You'd never be able to tell that someone 'd kicked it in," he said, as someone kicked it in.

The force of the blow was so great that the door came off its hinges, taking much of the surrounding framework with it.

Standing in the doorway was the most incredible display of sinews either of them had ever seen in their lives, including the awesome rabble from the previous day's visit.

"Who—" the innkeeper began, stepping back as the first bulbous figure stepped forward, crushing the remains of the Welcroft's door under his feet like a side of beef.

The man must have been about eight feet tall, and to say that he had muscles would've been the understatement of the Tri Age. He didn't *have* muscles; he *was* muscles. They were everywhere: his neck, shoulders, chest, arms, and legs. Even his face was flexing (so much so, in fact, that it was actually difficult to see his eyes). A thatch of dark hair worked overtime to cover his cannonball skull.

The second of the three was a good foot shorter than his extraordinary companion, and looked just like an ogre in a raincoat. He had long blond hair, and the kind of face that only a lifetime of head-butts would give you.

The third man was a dwarf, but unlike any dwarf the innkeeper had ever crossed paths with. It had a fat head, a network of scars, and hair sprouting up in random patches.

All three were dressed in rough slacks, and they all wore loose vests with the arms cut out. Despite the size of the hole they'd made in the wall of the inn, they had to enter one at a time. When they were all huddled inside, the innkeeper felt as if he were a herring trapped in a net full of whales.

"C-c-can I help you?" was all he could think of to say.

The first man extended a hand and held it straight (presumably, so the muscles around his wrist wouldn't fall out).

"I'm Mr. Big," he said, shaking the innkeeper's hand with such force that the man felt himself leaving the ground several times. "Nice to finally meet you."

"You too, v-very nice."

"This is Mr. Mediocre, an' Mr. Titch. We've come for our boy Loogie. Where is he?"

The innkeeper opened and shut his mouth a few times, then glanced at his wife. She was still looking at the pathetic remains of the door.

"We know the thievin' little wretch was 'ere," said Mr. Mediocre. "So I suggest you start talkin'."

The innkeeper nodded. "I, er, we, I mean *they*, took him."

Mr. Big blinked, causing the veins in his eyelids to start a judo match.

"Who took him?" he barked.

"Where?" echoed Mediocre. "When?"

Titch didn't say anything.

"He was here yesterday morning," the innkeeper managed, quickly adding, "I gave him the money I owed you."

Big nodded.

"WHO TOOK HIM?" he repeated.

"Two big barbarians," said his wife. She appeared to be in a daze, and her eyes hadn't left the floor.

"Not as well turned out as you lads," the innkeeper stated hurriedly. "But still a fair handful, if you know what I mean. They had a dwarf with 'em; might've been the leader."

"What 'appened?" Mr. Mediocre asked. The innkeeper noticed that he spoke without moving his lips.

"They, er, nicked one of my carts, then beat your man senseless and tied him to the back of it. I don't know where they were going, but they were definitely headed toward the Washin."

"That's all right," said Mediocre, smiling. "We've got a barge."

Mr. Big eyed the innkeeper carefully.

"You reckon he's telling the truth?" he said, glancing back at his companions.

They both gave a reluctant nod.

"I am, sir," the innkeeper bleated. "Absolutely the gods' own truth, sir."

"Yeah, well, we'll just have to see, won't we? Now, how many times has Loogie been here to collect my money?"

"T-twice, sir."

"An' you paid 'im both times?" Mediocre inquired.

"Er . . . yes, sir. All we could afford, sir."

Big nodded. "I thought so. Let's move. . . ."

Big snapped his fingers and the other two turned and headed out of the inn.

"Thanks for your help," he said to the innkeeper, making for the entrance hole himself. "An' don't worry yourself; I'll be collecting my own money from next month on. . . ."

The group sniggered as they loped into the distance.

Groan and Gordo were hacking their way back through the forest of Rintintetly. Gape walked a little ways behind the duo, occasionally fingering the wound on his neck. Although the bite didn't hurt anymore, he was still very conscious of it.

"Keep alert," Gordo warned, peering over his shoulder.

It had taken them the best part of the morning to find the path they'd used to enter the wood. Still, they'd managed to get a few hours' sleep, and now, at last, things were looking up. They could hear the rushing waters of the Washin in the distance. Nobody wanted to talk about the fire demon or the sky-spinner. In fact, nobody wanted to talk about anything that'd happened the previous day. Besides, there were more pressing matters. . . .

"I don't understand it," Gape said, kicking the odd branch as he strode along. "Why would she send us off after a lot of treasures that don't exist?"

"Yeah, right, don' make no sense," Groan bellowed, but he could've been talking about *anything*.

"It makes perfect sense," chirped the head of Loogie Lambontroff. "You've all been done up like a sack full of kippers."

"I think he's right," Gordo added. "I just can't work out for the life of me *why* the princess would have it in for all of us?"

"Maybe she didn't," Gape hazarded. "Maybe it's her father or something?"

"I ain't never done nothin' ta Phlegm," Groan roared.

"None of us have," Gordo agreed. "We've had our problems with Dullitch—"

"An' Legrash," Groan added.

"And Spittle, but never any truck with Phlegm."

The sound of the river was getting closer. Gape made a beeline for it, and the others followed.

"Curfew must've been pretty rattled when we broke out of his dungeons," Gordo reasoned, thinking aloud. "And I know his uncle *really* hated us. Hey, Groan, d'you remember Duke Modeset?"

Groan frowned with the effort of recollection. "Didn' 'e drop a cage over us when we saved them kids from tha' wizard?" he said.

"That's him," said Gordo. "Poisoned us too, you remember?"

"What about when *we* first met up?" Gape said. "You remember half-inching those jeweled swords from Legrash?"

"Yeah." Groan laughed. "We got a good price for 'em, an' all. Wha' 'bout that countin' howse we smashed up in Sneeze—when Chuckbuckle or wha'ever 'is name was came after us on 'is cart horse?"

There was a moment of awkward silence.

"You know," Gordo said. "We've probably upset a fair few nobles in our time."

"Me too," Gape muttered.

Groan swiped at an overhanging branch. "O' course we 'ave," he thundered. "What else is there?"

The trio emerged onto the eastern bank of the Washin, and Gape immediately began searching the ground.

Gordo and Loogie watched as the warrior hurried back and forth across the riverbank, shaking his head.

Groan frowned. "What's your problem?" he shouted.

"The boat!" Gape called back. "Someone's taken the boat!"

"Oh, is that what is was?" said Stump, suddenly emerging from the river with a wriggling fish on a stick. "I probably shouldn't have burned it then, eh?"

The ensuing silence was quickly disrupted.

"You did what?" Gape exclaimed, drawing both swords and striding toward the wildman.

"Sorry," said Stump, holding his hands out

apologetically. "But I needed to get a fire going, and I thought it was just boat-shaped wood."

"I'll let you in on a little secret," Gape muttered. "Wood formed in the shape of a boat is something we like to call . . . a BOAT."

"Like I said, I'm really sorry. There's a lot of it left. Did you lot have anything to do with the skyship that crashed into the river earlier? Frightened me out of my life, that did. I was gonna go looking for it, then I thought—"

"I know you!" Gordo said, recognizing the profile. "You're that weirdo from the Twelve: Stap, Strop, no, Stump, isn't it?" He turned to his companion. "You remember Stump, Groan? He was with young Jimmy that time, in the mountain."

Groan nodded. "Yeah, he dis'peared."

"So he did." Gordo laughed at the recollection. "Where'd you go, Stump?"

The wildman shrugged. "Fell down a hole, I think. Funny really, because I fell down a hole in the first place, ha-ha-ha-ha!"

"Whatever," Gape snapped, lowering his swords and slumping onto a nearby rock. "All I want to know is how we're planning to get across the river without a bloody boat!"

"Don't panic," Gordo told the warrior, as Stump led him toward the smoking wreckage of what had once been their boat. "I'm sure we can still make a decent raft."

"A raft?" Gape gasped. "When we had a perfectly good boat? We should throw this maniac in the river!"

"Thanks a lot," said Stump grumpily. "But I've had enough water for one lifetime."

He indicated the river and rolled his eyes.

Groan shrugged. "Match *your* bad 'xperiences 'gainst ours any day o' the week."

"I don't think so," Stump muttered, toasting his fish over the dying embers of his fire.

"Oh, yeah?" said Gordo, sitting down beside the wildman. "How's this? First we're conned into questing for nonexistent treasures by a lying princess—"

Gape cut in. "*Then* we rescue an innkeeper and his wife, get lumbered with a crazy gangster—"

"I resent that," said a voice.

"—who turns out to be a half-zombie twinling that won't die even when we decapitate it."

"*Then* we're cheated out of a riverboat crossing by the wily old maniac whose boat you just burned,"

Gordo went on. "Then—wait, I'm not finished—then we get attacked by archers, taken to the forgotten city of Wemeru, and have a right old kick off with people who've been dead longer than we've been alive. We end the day flying over Kazbrack Island in a pile of enchanted wood, pursued by fire demons and spat at by a giant volcano! Top that!"

Stump whistled between his teeth. "I can't top it," he said, as Groan took a seat at his side. "But how's this: I started the morning being pursued across a mean stretch of forest by a blue tiger. Then I got knocked unconscious and tied up by some crazy girl, who turns out to be a princess in disguise; then her and her maid get caught by a duke who shoots the tiger—"

"What princess?" Gape interrupted, glaring at the wildman with fiery eyes.

Stump shrugged. "I didn't catch her name," he managed. "But her father's the King of Phlegm."

"What DUKE?" Gordo asked, standing up and gripping the handle of his stout battle-axe.

"I think I heard her call him Modeset," said Stump. "But hang on a minute, the best bit's still to come—"

"MODESET!" Gordo muttered, staring at Gape

and Groan, who were also beginning to look decidedly concerned. "What's he doing in Phlegm?"

"Takin' over, by the looks of it." Stump laughed. "By the time I managed to escape on his royal coach, he'd had the king and his daughter dragged away by their own guards! Crazy, eh? Who'd have thought you could overthrow a king with words!"

There followed a sudden, terrible silence.

"What words in particular?" Gape asked, licking his lips as he saw Stump tucking into his fish.

The wildman finished his mouthful and grinned. "Well, from what I heard, he threatened to tell the other leaders that the princess'd interfered with his plan by trying to warn your big friend, here, about something. . . ."

All eyes turned to Groan, as the big barbarian flexed his muscles. "We've bin 'ad," he said.

"Yeah." Gordo nodded. "By bloody Modeset. We should've killed that vindictive little squirt when we busted out of Dullitch."

"Na, he'd 'ready bin exiled by then," Groan said, stealing a cut of Stump's fish for himself. Gordo and Gape followed suit.

"I know I'm not in the best position to contribute to all your intricate conspiracy talk," said the head of Loogie Lambontroff gruffly. "But would you mind including me in the food handouts, because I'm not quite dead, you know."

Gordo pressed a slice of fish against Loogie's lips, and peered balefully out at the river.

TWENTY

"I DON'T BELIEVE IT," Gordo said, peering out at the river. "We spend all afternoon lashing a raft together, and just when we finally complete the thing, we don't bloody need it."

"Eh?" Groan mumbled, raising an eyebrow.

"There's a barge coming," Gape translated. "And a decent-sized one at that."

"Let's have a look," Loogie muttered, annoyed that he couldn't scratch the itch beneath his nose.

"There's not much *to* see," Stump told him. "It's just a big red barge with something scrawled on the side of it."

"Let me see NOW!" screamed Loogie.

Gordo sighed, unhooked the head, and held it up toward the river.

"Satisfied?" the dwarf snapped.

"Yeah," said Loogie, smiling nervously. "But I'd get back in the woods if I were you."

Gape glanced at Groan, and they both stared at the trembling head.

"Why's that?" Gordo asked.

"Because that barge belongs to my boss, and he isn't a very nice man."

Groan shrugged.

"Yeah, well, neither are we," said Gape resentfully. "And we've had a really bad day."

"I'm *serious,*" Loogie's head intoned. "The best thing we can do is make a run for it. If we don't, they'll kill us ALL."

"Groan Teefgrit runs from no man," roared Groan.

"He's not kidding," Gordo added.

"Is it all going to kick off?" Stump inquired, always on the lookout for his own personal safety. "Because I've got places to go, you know—"

"Here, look after this," said Gordo, waddling over to the wildman and thrusting the head into his hands.

"Now, hang on—"

"Just be thankful that we're not handing you a sword," Gordo told him, unsheathing his battle-axe.

Groan and Gape drew their blades at the same moment. They could both vaguely make out figures moving around on the flat deck of the barge.

"It's Mr. Big," Loogie chattered, sweat beginning to form on his brow. "He's probably looking for me . . . and he never travels alone."

"How many of them are there, then?" Gape asked, climbing onto his rock to gain a better vantage point.

"Can't see," said Groan. The giant barbarian had already assumed battle stance.

"There's three," said Stump, who lived and died by the strength of his eyesight. He pointed at Groan: "One guy who looks about your height, one not much smaller, and a dwarf. They're all armed."

"Look, we don't actually have to fight, do we?" Gordo said doubtfully. "I mean, if he's *your* boss—"

"I see where you're going with that," said the head of Loogie Lambontroff. "Only problem is, I sort of ran out on him about six weeks ago, and I've been freelancing a bit with his customers. I doubt whether he'll throw his arms around me, not that he could even if he wanted to. . . ."

Gape squinted at the barge. "You reckon they're

all armed?" he said to Stump. "Can you see what they're armed *with*?"

The wildman nodded. "Two have got swords, and it looks like the big one's got a pistol."

"How come every scumbucket's got a pistol, all of a sudden?" Gordo spat, staring gloomily at his battle-axe. "I don't know, some bloke in Legrash invents a hand-banger and suddenly you can't get away from 'em."

"You're telling me!" said Loogie, who was a good two hundred years older than anybody else. "It was the same thing with crossbows, you know."

Stump sniggered at the remark, and was about to give his own opinions on the danger posed by ballistics, when a piece of lead shot took a chunk out of his shoulder.

"Ahhhhh!"

The wildman fell, unintentionally throwing Loogie high into the air, as Groan and Gordo dived for the safety of the riverbank.

Gape had dropped one of his swords and was spinning around in a circle with the other, like a particularly adept shot-putter. Faster and faster he went, every muscle straining with the effort. Finally, he released his remaining sword, which shot out across the water like a rogue missile.

There was a distant scream, and the biggest figure on the barge toppled backward into the water. His two companions immediately dived in, but it soon became apparent that they weren't planning to linger around the barge looking for him. They were heading straight for the shore.

"Stay down," Gape warned Stump, who was rolling around in agony and probably didn't need the advice. At least he'd managed to catch the head on its way down.

Groan strode down the beach, splashed into the shallow water, and actually plucked Mr. Mediocre out of the river while the man was still swimming. He quickly smacked the sword out of Mediocre's hand, grabbed him by the arm, and swung him toward Gape, who slugged the gangster in the face with his free hand and raised his sword for a vertical slash. Unfortunately, he didn't get the chance to swing it.

Mediocre threw three punches in quick succession, each explosively well judged, and all on target. Gape staggered back, as surprised at the strength of his opponent as he was that the man had survived a Gape "face-slammer."

Gordo Goldeaxe, at the far end of the bank, was

having serious problems. The dwarf that had leaped from the water had disarmed him with comparative ease and was now ruthlessly slashing at his armor with a gleaming short sword.

Groan turned away from the water, trying to decide who was more in need of his help. The answer was obvious: Gape was being totally out-classed by his opponent. Groan grinned and stomped off to help Gordo. He was almost upon the two dwarves when Mr. Big waded out of the Washin and clouted him hard in the face.

Groan fell back onto the beach as the gangster pulled Gape's sword out of his stomach and tossed it aside like a matchstick.

"Now I'm bitter," he said.

Mr. Big leaped into the air as Groan tried for a leg-sweep. Then he dragged the giant barbarian to his feet and head-butted him right between the eyes, using the time bought by Groan's momentary con-fusion to kick the warrior's broadsword away. It slid to a halt a little way down the bank.

Mr. Big sniffed. Then he brought up a heavy knee and, as Groan doubled up, chopped him roughly on the neck. The barbarian went down, hard.

"The bigger they are, eh? Ha!"

The gangster gave the prone warrior a gap-toothed grin and turned to see how his cohorts were doing. Thankfully, the scene was a pleasing one: both Mediocre and Titch were winning their respective struggles.

"Good on you, boys," he shouted. Then he turned back and, to his surprise, came face-to-face with Groan.

"Is 'at all you got?" the barbarian thundered and drove a fist like bunched steel into Mr. Big's stomach.

Stump, meanwhile, was attempting to shoulder himself along the bank, dragging his new companion behind him.

"Maybe my twinling can help," the head muttered. "Get me angry; get me angry!"

"And how am I supposed to do that?" Stump complained, clutching at his bleeding wound.

"I don't know—bang me on a rock or something!"

Stump looked around, found a flat stone, and slammed the head against it.

"Harder!"

A second time.

"Harder! Harder!"

A third.

"Ow! Not that bloody hard! You're flaming use-less!"

"And you're nothing but a damn nuisance!"

"Yeah? I'd do you up a treat—"

Stump swore under his breath and lobbed the head over his shoulder. He didn't see where it landed.

Mr. Mediocre raised a fist and slammed it down across Gape's back. The warrior moaned, collapsed to the ground, and drove his hand into his boot. When he brought it out again, he was wielding a blade.

Mediocre grabbed Gape's wrist, but the barbar-ian was stronger: he forced the gangster's hand back toward him and slashed a deep wound across his chest. Then he turned Mediocre around and drove him headfirst into the Washin.

Groan had given Mr. Big six of his best shots, but the man had simply shrugged them off. Now he was blocking every blow, a filthy grin pasted across his face.

He ducked the last of Groan's punches and caught the barbarian with one of his own.

"You're a big lad," he muttered. "But yer punch ain't worth spit."

He pulled a pistol from his sodden suit, flipped it over, and smacked Groan in the face with it. As the warrior fell onto his knees, he reached out for Gape's sword.

Mr. Big stamped on his hand. "No thanks," he said. "I've had that sword in my stomach, and I'm not in any hurry to get it ba—"

Mr. Big stopped talking.

An identical sword had sprouted from his rib cage.

"You're quite right," said a voice behind him. "My swords *do* seem to like you."

Mr. Big spun around in a state of bewildered shock, and grabbed Gape by the throat . . .

. . . just as Groan lost his temper.

The barbarian unfolded like a deck chair. Then he wrenched Mr. Big away from his brother, withdrew Gape's sword from the man's ribs, and punched him with all his might.

The gangster staggered back and collapsed in a disheveled heap: he didn't get up again.

Gape took his sword from Groan and reached down to snatch up the other.

Groan gulped some air. "Fanks fo' the 'elp."

"Don't mention it."

"I would've 'ad 'im anyway."

"Yes, I know that."

"I'm jus' sayin'."

"Fine."

They both peered over at Gordo, who had turned the tide on his fellow dwarf and was driving Mr. Titch back down the beach with his own sword. It certainly didn't seem as though he needed any assistance.

Groan glanced down at Big, who was lying still.

"What 'appen'd to that uvver one?" he said.

"Swam away," said Gape. "The cowardly rat."

He looked on, bewildered, as Groan suddenly bolted down the riverbank and dived into the Washin.

"What are you doing?" he shouted, as Stump appeared beside him with an incredibly indignant head.

"I think he's trying to get to Mediocre before Mediocre gets to the barge," he guessed.

And he was right.

Groan had adopted a smooth underwater breaststroke in order to counter the gangster's frenzied crawl. Mediocre reached the barge first but, despite his head start, there wasn't a lot in it.

Gape, Gordo, and Stump watched as Groan

climbed onto the barge and began to struggle with Mr. Mediocre. Loogie would've watched, but he was facing the wrong way.

"Go on, Groan!"

"Give him hell!"

"Low blow, low blow!"

"Can somebody please turn me 'round?"

A series of blows were exchanged before the gangster toppled into the water and floated away. Groan strode to the far end of the barge and began to steer it slowly toward the east bank.

"So," Stump said, as Gordo proffered a rough bandage for his shoulder. "Are we going for a trip along the river, then?"

"No," said Gape sternly. "We're going to rescue a princess, overthrow an evil dictator, and sack a city."

"Ah, right." Stump flashed a grim smile. "Still," he said. "You've got to laugh, haven't you?"

PART THREE

THE FIGHT FOR PHLEGM

TWENTY-ONE

TWO NIGHTS LATER, in the converted hall of records at Phlegm Keep, Susti wriggled her arms in an attempt to loosen the pressure on her wrists. No use: the manacles were fastened tight. Still, it could've been worse: at least they had platforms to stand on.

She peered across at her father and Bronwyn, who were both, unfathomably, asleep. Susti couldn't understand how *anybody* could sleep with their arms raised high above them.

She focused on the king.

"Psst!"

Nothing.

"Father!"

At first she thought the king might wake; then he began to snore.

Susti sighed, as the door to the hall creaked open and Pegrand limped inside.

"Good evening, milady," he said, holding his ribs with one hand and a tray of goblets in the other. "Thought I might bring you all some water?"

Susti nodded. "Are you okay?"

"Yes, milady. My chest is a bit battered and my leg's been better, but otherwise I'm fine."

"Hmm . . . you really shouldn't have betrayed me, you know. I mean, I understand why you did what you did, but honestly"—Susti shook her head—"No. I'm not talking to you. You'll only repeat everything I tell you to Modeset."

Pegrand nodded. "Probably, milady. I'm sorry."

"Yes, so am I," Susti said regretfully. "Sorry that you've spent practically *all* of your life serving someone who doesn't appreciate your loyalty, someone who only thinks of thrones and power, someone who'd rather fawn over a makeshift general than tend to the wounds of his own faithful manservant. I'm sorry for *you*, Pegrand."

"Well, milady, I appreciate the thought, but it really is *my* business."

He hobbled up the narrow flight of stone steps to the length of wall where Susti was confined, and raised the goblet to her lips. When she'd drunk her fill, he replaced the goblet on the tray . . . and looked up again.

"Which one would you have married?" he asked, his expression earnest in the glimmering torchlight.

Susti frowned. "What?"

"The Teethgrits," Pegrand muttered. "If there *was* no plan and you really meant to marry, which warrior would you have chosen for a husband?"

Susti thought for a moment, then managed a noncommittal shrug.

"Neither," she said. "I like my men modest . . . and preferably loyal to a heart, not a purse. Even if you weren't a hundred years too old, *you'd* never do."

Pegrand's face flushed, and he hobbled across to wake the king from his slumber. Susti watched the manservant raise a goblet for her father and Bronwyn, and wondered if thirty-nine was really as old as all that.

"Right," Gordo said, surveying the vast array of weapons and armor that they'd unloaded from the gangster's barge the night before. "We've got ten longbows, six hundred arrows."

"Firty swords, five axes," Groan added, brows

meeting as he tried to do the math in his head.

"Ten crossbows, fifty bolts," said Gape.

"One empty pistol," Stump said, tossing the spent weapon to the grass.

"And a head," Loogie finished, speaking from his resting place atop the crossbow pile.

"How many guards d'you reckon they've got in Phlegm?" Gordo said to Gape.

The warrior shrugged. "Who knows? Judging by the arena turnout, I'd say more than one hundred, less than three."

"That's still too many," said Stump, suddenly wondering why he was still with the group, and making a conscious decision to leg it at the first available opportunity.

"Not if we attack 'em in the small 'ours," Groan thundered. "Like we did in Sneeze, one time."

Gordo nodded. "Mind you," he said reflectively. "The Sneeze defenses weren't up to much, were they? In fact, as I recall, there was only the baron and his nephew . . . and they turned on each other. This is a different kettle of fish. You know what Modeset's like; he's—"

"—not expecting us ever to come back," Gape concluded, a smug grin developing on his face. "So when we attack tonight, his troops won't be ready for us." The warrior stared at Gordo thoughtfully for a long time, as if they both shared the same vision but neither one could be bothered to spell it out for the other.

Finally, it was the head of Loogie Lambontroff who spoke.

"So what you do is, you split into two groups: one takes as many men off the wall as they possibly can, and the other tries to breach the main gate with a ram of some kind."

Gordo nodded and thrust a finger at Gape. "You and Groan chop down a tree and charge at the main gate—"

"Why do we—"

"Because you're the strongest. Stump and I will handle the ballistics."

"Will we?" the wildman moaned, an edge of desperation to his voice. "Oh, good; I'm . . . thrilled."

Night had washed over the battlements of Phlegm Keep and was struggling valiantly to hold off the morrow.

In the banqueting hall, a midnight feast was

taking place. The long table, loaded down with roast chicken, thick cuts of pork, and a selection of heavy bread rolls, was occupied by three figures at its far end.

"Try the chicken, Pegrand," Modeset advised, accepting a plate of pork from General Crikey. "It'll help get your strength back."

The manservant self-consciously touched a hand to his bruised ribs, and managed a depressed nod.

"Good man," Modeset continued, turning back to Crikey. "You can expect a lot more feasts like this with me in charge, General."

"Splendid, lordship." The officer smiled.

Pegrand glared at him.

"I suppose we should hold some kind of *internal* coronation," said the duke. "And maybe an official promotion ceremony for you, General."

Crikey nodded eagerly, munching on a chicken leg.

He was about to take a drink from one of the silver wine goblets, when the door to the hall flew open and a junior guard hurried in.

"What is it?" Crikey asked, rising from his chair.

"We're under attack, General," the boy panted. "We've got twenty men down at the city gate, and the sentries on the east wall are reporting heavy losses."

"Do we have any idea who the attackers are?" Modeset demanded.

The guard smiled nervously. "It's difficult to say, lordship," he said, staring down at his feet. "It's still dark out there. Whoever they are, they're attacking in two separate bursts. We've got arrows flying in from the east, and there's some kind of battering ram on the city gate."

Modeset nodded. "I see. You are dismissed, boy." He turned to Crikey, whose hands were beginning to shake. "I wonder, General: what is the most powerful ballistic weapon you have at your disposal?"

Crikey thought for a moment. "The sentry harpoon, Your Highness." He smiled. "The men call it the Assoonas Harpoon, because *Assoonas* it hits you, you're dead."

Modeset leaped to his feet.

"Show me," he said, "and get me a pistol too." As he and the general headed out into the corridor, neither of them noticed that Pegrand had also quietly slipped away. . . .

Stump was unexpectedly turning out to be the best marksman Gordo had ever seen. The wildman had yet to miss a target, even though he fired off each arrow with his eyes closed. Admittedly, most of his success was due to the fact that the head of Loogie Lambontroff was on the tree branch next to him, guiding his every shot.

"Left, down, fire! Reload. Left, left, down, right, fire! Reload. Down, down, down, left, now! Reload."

"Will you shut up?" Gordo snapped, fumbling his own shot because of the distraction. "I'm trying to concentrate over here."

They were both going for leg shots, trying to keep any casualties to a minimum; but more and more guards were hurrying round from the other sides of the wall, and shooting with no such precision.

"We're gonna be dead meat if we stay here much longer," Stump warned, uncovering his eyes long enough to glance around him. "This tree's shedding branches like autumn leaves. We've got to make a move."

The wildman began to descend to the ground.

"Two more shots," Gordo promised, and went back to his crossbow, picking off one of the new guards and wounding another. Then he threw the weapon to Stump and climbed down after him.

* * *

Groan and Gape, shields held high over their heads with one hand and each supporting one half of the tree they'd felled with the other, took a tenth run-up at the gate and slammed their wooden ram into it.

There was a series of muffled yelps from beyond the great door, and they both heard the sound of many feet being driven back.

"Couple more should do it," Gape cried, as an arrow sprouted from his right arm.

The guard captains had been sending men out from some secret entrance to attack them at intervals, but none of them seemed to know how to fight, and the two barbarians had swatted them away like flies, using their shield arms to fling them down the hillside. Most, Gape noticed, were simply taking one shot and running away. Pathetic.

Still, more were arriving every few minutes, and those that did were becoming bolder, hovering around the ram and attempting to drive blades into the Teethgrit armor. Thankfully, their aim was poor and Mr. Big's armor was really, *really* good.

Groan and Gape dashed forward once more.

An eleventh thundering jolt hit the gate.

Back.

Back.

Back.

FORWARD.

A twelfth, and the gate gave a sickening creak . . . and crashed to the ground.

Groan and Gape dropped the log and stared in disbelief at the sight that greeted them.

Beyond the portal, there was a long line of soldiers, all of whom had dropped their weapons, and all of whom had parted to reveal a straight road through Phlegm . . .

. . . leading up to the keep.

Groan and Gape glanced at each other, and stepped boldly forward.

TWENTY-TWO

"THE CITY'S under attack, and I've changed my mind," Pegrand muttered, reaching up to unlock Susti's manacles and lifting the princess down onto her feet. "It's not right, *any* of it . . . and you were spot on about my not being appreciated."

Susti grinned down at the manservant as he untied her feet, then she and Pegrand set to work on the bonds of the sleeping king.

"To think: I've stood by him through thick and thin. All that business with the virgin sacrifices, the ratastrophe catastrophe, even the Yowler foul-up, and what thanks do I get? It makes me mad—"

"And so it should," Susti said, as Pegrand finished working on the king's bonds and hurried over to Bronwyn.

King Phew stared blearily around him. "W-what's happening?"

"We're getting out, Father."

Phew slumped onto his knees. "Not again," he begged. "Please, I'm not up to it."

Susti smiled warmly. "Relax," she said. "The duke has other things to worry about."

Bronwyn shook out her hair as Pegrand helped her down.

"Thank you," she said, rushing over to Susti and wiping some dust from her mistress's dress. "Are we on the run again, ma'am?"

"I'm afraid so, Bronwyn. We just don't quite know where *to*, this time."

"I do," said Pegrand distractedly. "We're going to *deal* with the duke."

"Groan Teethgrit," Modeset said to the general, from their vantage point atop the battlements of the keep. "I assume we have the wildman to thank for his return. Hmm . . . remind me to hunt down those two guards and execute them, would you?"

"Yes, sir," Crikey growled, watching as the Teethgrit brothers marched up the deserted street toward the keep.

"Tell me, General," Modeset continued, turning his head ever so slightly to consider the officer's face. "Why is it that your men are simply *allowing* them through?"

"I don't know, sir."

"Can it be that their allegiance is even more easily swayed at night than it is during the daytime?"

"I—"

"Don't have clue," Modeset finished. "No, you don't, but you're about to learn, General. You see, if you want something done in this life, generally speaking, you have to do it yourself."

The duke just managed to raise the giant sentry harpoon, and hefted it onto the buttress. Crikey swallowed a few times and massaged his aching neck.

"Highness, are you absolutely—"

Modeset took aim . . .

"—sure?"

. . . and fired.

Gordo Goldeaxe had run from a lot of guards in his life, but he'd never run *after* any before.

"Where are they going?" Stump asked, hurrying along behind him with the head of Loogie Lambontroff bouncing at his waist.

Gordo shrugged and quickened his pace. "How should I know?" he said. "There's obviously something far more exciting going on at the main gate. Let's hope they broke through, eh?"

"Yeah," Stump said, jogging along. "Mind you, they might end up facing moeraaaaghhhhhhhhhh!"

"Mo who?" said Gordo, who suddenly realized he was running on his own, and backtracked to the edge of a very deep pit.

"Stump?"

"Yeah," came a distant voice.

Gordo shook his head. "I don't believe it," he said. "Do you go looking for these holes, or what?"

His words echoed.

"No, I was too busy talking to you to see the damn thing!"

"Can you climb out?"

"Er—"

There came the noise of frantic scrambling.

"—No. Sorry."

"But you've got the rest of the arrows!"

"I know; but there's not a hell of a lot I can do about it now."

"Terrific," Gordo shouted. "Absolutely terrific. I'll just leave you down there, then. Shall I?"

"Probably your best bet," Stump yelled back. "I—wait—what a stroke of luck! There's a tunnel down here. Looks like it leads away from the city. I might just follow it. . . ."

Gordo rolled his eyes. "Why do I get the feeling I won't see you again for a while?"

"I don't know what you mean!" Stump shouted. "Still, looking on the bright side, at least I've got company."

"Oh, joy," echoed the voice of Loogie Lambontroff.

"I'll see you around," Stump called again, but Gordo had already gone.

"You would've have thought," Modeset said, shoving the harpoon toward General Crikey, "that the chances of him catching that harpoon were about five hundred to one against. It just shows you."

"Er, with respect, Highness, he didn't catch the harpoon—it stuck in his armor and he pulled it out."

Modeset shrugged. "Well, even *so*—"

They both glanced down at Groan Teethgrit, who had taken the drawbridge across the moat and was advancing on the keep's portcullis, bending the duke's harpoon in half. His brother had already set to work on the portcullis, jamming his swords through the grid in an effort to draw the mechanism's chain toward him.

Crikey returned his attention to the duke, who was staring expectantly at him.

"Well?" Modeset said.

"Well what, Highness?"

"Reload the damn crossbow! Grief, and I thought Pegrand was slow—"

"Actually, I'm not that slow, milord," said a voice, and Modeset felt a hand lift the pistol from his belt. He spun around and came face-to-face with the barrel end.

General Crikey was so shocked that he dropped the harpoon over the wall.

Groan peered up at the keep's battlements, saw the harpoon plummeting down, and dived at Gape, knocking his brother away from the portcullis in the nick of time.

"Careful," he warned the warrior as he pulled him back onto his feet. "They're frowin' stuff down now."

"Thanks, brother."

"F'get it; we're even."

Gape nodded. "Look," he said, pointing at the portcullis. "I got the chain through; we can raise it."

"Yeah, I reckon—NO!"

Groan saw the danger just in time: a pot of boiling oil had been rigged up to fall when the portcullis was raised.

The giant barbarian leaped sideways, attempting to grab hold of his brother's arm in the process. He failed.

The oil poured down over Gape, who let out a shocked scream and collapsed to the ground.

Groan, meanwhile, had tripped in his hurry to escape the oil and had toppled over the drawbridge, where he hung mere feet above the shark-infested moat. For a moment, he simply hung there, motionless, not wanting to raise himself because of the sight he would inevitably see when he did.

Eventually, the mental images of a crispy-fried Gape became too much, and he pulled himself back onto the drawbridge . . .

. . . to see Gape standing under the keep's raised portcullis, nonchalantly wiping oil from his shoulders.

" 'ere," Groan said, not able to the stop the relief from showing in his smile. "I fort you was burned."

Gape looked himself up and down. "Tell me

about it," he said. "There was a slight pain at first, and then . . . nothing. I guess that fire demon did me a favor when it bit me."

"Yeah," Groan boomed. "I reckon it did."

"What on Illmoor do you think you're doing?" Modeset demanded, turning red with rage as Pegrand stuck the pistol under his chin.

"I'm taking back the kingdom," his manservant said.

Susti, Bronwyn, and the king appeared on the buttresses. They were all armed with crossbows.

"Y-you can't be serious!" Modeset spat. "What is the meaning of this treachery?"

Pegrand sniffed. "Treachery is easy," he said, nodding toward Crikey. "Just ask him."

"B-but why, damn it!"

"Because I'm fed up with you, milord, and I'm sick to the back teeth of your stupid, whining voice in my head. I've stood by your side through thick and thin, followed your every whim, and faced one flamin' calamity after another." He snatched hold of the duke's robe. "And now I can honestly, finally say, *milord*, that your stinking rotten attitude gets right on my tits."

Modeset was shaking with embarrassment. "Y-you've never said anything before."

"No," Pegrand agreed with a sigh. "That's because I could never get a word in edgewise." He tightened his grip on the gun and pulled back the linchpin. "But now the tables are turned, aren't they? Because I can talk all I want, and you have to listen!"

Modeset gulped.

"I know," Pegrand observed. "Horrible, isn't it? Now move your sorry excuse for a—"

"Wait!" Modeset held up a placating hand. "Pegrand, if you turn that gun around, I promise I'll reward you well. . . ."

The manservant glanced behind him at the king, and at Bronwyn. Then he saw Susti smiling confidently, and returned his attention to the duke.

"I'm sorry, milord," he said. "No deal."

Modeset, however, had caught the flicker in his servant's eye.

"I don't believe this!" he exclaimed, a grin suddenly spreading across his face. "You wouldn't be falling for the good princess, would you, Pegrand?"

The manservant swallowed. "I don't know what you're talking about, mil—"

"You *are*, aren't you? You're actually in love with Sissy."

"It's Susti," said Susti, flushing.

"Have you gone completely out of your mind?" Modeset laughed. "What on Illmoor makes you think that a beautiful young girl would look twice at an aging ferret like you?"

Pegrand glanced from Susti's smiling face to Modeset's mocking scowl, and took a deep breath. "Flicka looked twice at you, milord."

Every muscle in Modeset's face dropped.

"I—"

"Well, didn't she?"

"As you will recall, Pegrand," the duke said deliberately. "That relationship didn't exactly work out."

"Yes, milord, and that was because you spent too much time and energy hankering after your lost kingdom. It's comical, really; you turned your back on the one girl who actually thought something of you."

"How dare—"

The trapdoor to the roof exploded outward, and Groan Teethgrit erupted from below, broadsword at the ready. Gape leaped out behind him, brandishing his blades in similar fashion.

There were a few seconds of brief confusion as Susti, Bronwyn, and the king made way for the warriors. It turned out to be just enough time for Modeset to seize the initiative: he swiftly snatched the pistol from Pegrand, then kicked him to the floor, and leveled the weapon at Groan.

"The mighty Groan Teethgrit," he said, stepping over the prone manservant. "Long time, no see."

Groan twirled his sword and nodded. "I never fanked you fer poisonin' me an' droppin' a cage on me 'ead."

Modeset grinned. "Well," he said. "Now you have the perfect opportunity. Thank away, you moron!"

Gape raised his swords and lowered them again, as General Crikey produced a minicrossbow from his belt and pointed it in his specific direction.

Nobody moved.

"So what do we do now?" Modeset chirped.

Groan shrugged. "Shoot me," he rumbled. "If ya got the guts."

There was a moment of silence, then Modeset shook his head.

"I don't *murder*," he said. "I'm a duke; I have people to do that sort of thing for me. General, shoot that man!"

"I can't, sir!" Crikey bleated. "I'm covering the other one."

"Pegrand." Modeset looked long and hard at the manservant, came to a swift decision, and threw him the pistol. "Redeem yourself!"

Pegrand snatched the weapon out of the air, panicked, and did what he thought was best. He tossed it to Susti.

The princess caught the pistol, grinned, and leveled it, pointing the weapon at everyone on the battlements in turn.

"No one is going to kill *anyone*, Duke Modeset," she said. "There's been enough bloodshed on your behalf already."

"Not yet, there ain't," said Groan.

The giant barbarian raised his sword and stepped toward Modeset.

"Now, hold on—" said the duke.

"Get back!" warned Susti.

"Nah," Groan boomed. "He's gonna pay fer sendin' me off after stuff that don't exist."

"It's not just *me* you have to thank for that," Modeset waffled.

Groan kept moving, but his brow was furrowed. "Eh?"

"They were all in on it: Phlegm, Legrash, Spittle, Sneeze, Dullitch! And you've only got yourself to blame. You, your spineless brother, and that cursed dwarf. You're a curse on this entire continent."

"An' you're dead meat," said Groan, swinging the mighty broadsword in an experimental arc.

"I said STOP!" Susti demanded.

Groan turned his head to look at her. "I don' like you no more," he said. "You're a *liar.*"

"Oh, don't blame *her,*" Modeset said, regaining the warrior's attention. "She didn't know her little speech was faked."

"I suppose that was your idea," Gape muttered, his gaze still resting firmly on Crikey's crossbow. "Still, the sweet princess served her purpose, didn't she?"

"Yes," Susti snapped. "Not that she'd ever consider wedding a pair of boneheads like you and your brainless brother." She stomped over the battlements and, to everyone's surprise, thrust the pistol back into Modeset's hands. "Go ahead, kill each other. I've met plenty of half-wits before, but never in my life have I encountered people who'd qualify for the quarter-wit grade."

Modeset raised the pistol.

Groan raised his sword.

"We are at an impasse," said the duke solemnly. "I'll die if you bring that sword down, but you'll die with me."

"Likewise," said Crikey, staring at Gape.

"So I'd like to make a suggestion, if I may."

Gordo Goldeaxe appeared at the trapdoor and staggered out onto the battlements, puffing and panting in the early morning air.

"Wh-what's going on?" he said.

"Believe it or not," Susti said. "They're all trying to predict who will kill who."

Gordo nodded. "Any luck?"

"Yes," Susti said, rolling her eyes. "They've realized they'll all kill each other."

"That doesn't sound good," the dwarf admitted.

"Gordo, isn't it?" Modeset cried, trying to peer around Groan's shoulder and keep his pistol steady at the same time. "Good old Gordo Goldeaxe. I was just telling your friend, here, that nobody will profit if everyone dies."

Gordo spotted the pistol. "You're right, Modeset," he said. "Even Groan's not that stupid."

"I might be," Groan bellowed, his sword remaining firmly aloft. "He ain't talkin' 'is way out o' this one."

"I promise you, Gordo," the duke shouted. "My plan is foolproof, and I swear that nobody on these battlements—with the possible exception of the king—will go home empty-handed."

Groan shook his head. "'Sall jus' words."

But Gordo's appetite for gold had been whetted. The little dwarf crossed the battlements in record time, leaping between the enemies with his axe raised.

"Drop your weapons," he said, looking from one to the other.

"Nah."

"No."

"DROP THEM."

"He'll strike me down."

"An' 'e'll shoot me."

"NOW!"

Groan lowered his sword . . . and Modeset shot him.

TWENTY-THREE

GROAN SAW a shadow move in front of him. He thrust out his sword, and felt pain in his leg: intense pain. His vision clouded and he collapsed onto his knees.

A second shot rang out. There was a brief *ping*, and Groan buckled backward, folding onto his back with his legs underneath him.

There were several shouts and a distant splash.

Someone gasped.

Groan's eyes rolled in his head . . .

. . . and then darkness overcame him.

General Crikey dropped the crossbow, staggered back, and gazed downward: both of Gape's swords were embedded in his chest. He looked up again, gave a strange smile, and sank slowly to the ground.

Gape, on his knees a few yards away, gasped with relief. The arrow had barely glanced his shoulder. It stuck out of the wall behind him, resonating like a twanged ruler.

Susti lowered her hands and checked that her father and Bronwyn were still standing. Then she hurried across to Pegrand, who was leaning over the keep's battlements, staring into the moat. His shoulders were trembling.

"It-it happened t-too f-fast," he managed. "I c-couldn't catch him."

Susti pulled the manservant back and peered over the edge herself. There was something floating in the water, and a quick head count told her who it was.

"Listen," she said, turning to the manservant and firmly grasping his arm. "It wasn't your fault."

Pegrand's eyes had filled with tears.

"B-but I-I-I—"

"You knocked his hand down," said Gordo. The dwarf was crouched beside Groan, tying a tourniquet he'd ripped from his jerkin around the barbarian's bleeding leg. His friend, it seemed, had lost consciousness. "And a good job, too: that first shot would've gone straight through Groan's chest."

Susti steered Pegrand away from the battlements, but the manservant wrestled free.

"You killed him!" he screamed, diving at the unconscious warrior. "You killed my master!"

Gordo leaped up to intercept the manservant, and with Gape's help, managed to force him to the ground.

"Listen to me!" the dwarf shouted into Pegrand's ear. "Modeset killed himself!"

"You're lying!"

"I'm not! You knocked his hand down, but he went for another shot. The second one rebounded off Groan's collar, hit Modeset in the face, and he fell. I'm TELLING you."

Pegrand stopped struggling. At Gordo's insistence, Gape released his grip on the manservant's legs and moved away from him. Eventually, the dwarf followed suit, leaving Pegrand a sad and lonely figure lying on the stones.

Susti stepped forward and helped him to his feet. As she was guiding the manservant toward the trapdoor, there came the distinct sound of whistling steel, and a blur shot past her.

"Argh!"

King Phew soared backward and crashed into the

wall of the keep's solitary scout tower, a giant broadsword protruding from the neck of his gold chain.

"I'm sick an' tired o' you damn lords," said Groan, shoving Gordo aside as he limped across the battlements. The barbarian came to a standstill, staring blearily at the king, while Susti, still supporting Pegrand, screamed for the city guard.

"It-it was Modeset's idea," Phew spluttered, as Groan gripped his shaking jaw.

"I don' care; you're all as bad as each uvver."

"GUARDS!" Susti screamed.

"It's no good, my dear," the king managed, talking out of the corner of his mouth. "They're about as loyal as a pack of pirates."

"Release my father," Susti pleaded, "and he'll give you the city."

Groan suddenly stopped menacing the king, and his great big cannonball head swiveled around to face the princess.

"He'll what?"

"He'll give you the Phlegmian throne," Susti said, glaring at the king. "Won't you, Father?"

"I will," said King Phew, massaging his jaw when Groan had finally released it. "It's yours. That is, if you want it."

Gordo tried to step forward, but found Gape's foot barring the way.

"This bedda no' be a trick," Groan warned the king, jabbing a finger into his eye for good measure. "I'll kill ya, 'f it is."

"It's no trick," Susti called. "My father is old, and his guards are disloyal. The city is full of rich, fat merchants who never go outside unless there's something in it for them. Now, if someone like *you* were on the throne, Phlegm would really become a city to be reckoned with—those other *vile* lords wouldn't *dare* attack you."

Groan glanced back at Gordo, who was nodding his head vigorously.

Gape didn't look so sure. "What's in it for me?" he said, slapping his chest. King Phew tried to speak, but Groan clamped a hand over his mouth.

"I'll give you one o' them floppy 'ats," he said.

Gape frowned. "What?"

"You know, them big floppy 'ats you give ta rich folk."

"You don't mean a deerstalker?"

"Nah."

"I think he means a knighthood," said Gordo, shaking his head.

"Yeah, thassit. You can 'ave one o' them."

"And me?" Gordo said, an expectant grin playing on his lips.

Groan thought for a moment. "You can be me guard boss."

"Oh," Gordo said noncommittally, but his mind was racing. At last, he thought, a job where people can't look down on me.

"All righ'," Groan boomed, turning back to the king. "I'll take it, but first I'm gonna get them lords what plowed 'ginst me."

"It's *plotted,* Your Majesty," Gordo corrected him. "But I'm right with you on that one."

TWENTY-FOUR

THREE WEEKS LATER, an eagle swooped to land on the sturdy battlements of Phlegm Keep.

Lord Phew, the keep's newly appointed custodian, had been awaiting the return of the messenger birds for several days. He was informed of the eagle's arrival by his apprentice, and quickly hurried to the roof to greet it. By the time he arrived, three more birds had gathered upon the battlements, each bearing their own burdens.

The former king bustled over to the first messenger and hurriedly retrieved the piece of parchment attached to its leg. He read it through twice before moving on to the next bird and following the same procedure. Eventually, having viewed all the messages, he dismissed the birds to their various quarters and turned to head back inside the keep.

He was halfway there when a figure stepped out of the shadows.

Phew started.

"M-my lord," he said. "You frightened the life out of me! I didn't realize you were up here. . . ."

A shrug. "You've heard from the other members, Majesty?"

Phew nodded. "They're all coming, my lord. And please don't call me Majesty—I'm not a king anymore. I'm just a lord, like yourself." He smiled. "Are you absolutely sure you want to go through with this?"

Duke Pegrand Marshall nodded. "Absolutely, *Lord* Phew. I don't think your daughter would ever agree to marry me if I didn't."

TWENTY-FIVE

THE VILLAGE of Shadewell was unaccountably quiet as Baron Muttknuckles rode in on his "royal" donkey. The streets were deserted and a light rain was beginning to fall from the leaden sky. Every now and then, a curtain would twitch, a door would slam, or some smudgy, inquisitive face would appear at a window.

Muttknuckles muttered under his breath as a coach rattled past, bearing the grand seal of Dullitch. It slowed down a little way in front, and Viscount Curfew appeared at the window.

"Can you believe this?" the nobleman snapped. "Twice in one year! I'm telling you, Modeset had better have a damn good reason for this summoning."

"I agree," said Earl Visceral, emerging on the far side of the Dullitch coach on his own imperial steed.

"I can't understand why he couldn't have said whatever he needed to say by ravensage. Those birds are even faster than carrier pigeons. And what's all this 'no guards' business? I'm telling you, the man's getting paranoid."

"Have you not brought guards with you?"

Visceral smiled. "I have thirty men on the edge of Shinbone forest. You?"

Curfew gave half a shrug. "Eighty, a mile or so outside the village. There's something distinctly odd about this meet—"

"Who cares?" Muttknuckles grumbled. "As long as it gets me out of Sneeze, I don't give a monkey's."

The three rode in silence for a time, Visceral and Curfew purposely slowing to keep pace with the baron.

"A bit quiet, isn't it?" the earl said, peering around him as if he'd only just noticed the silence.

"Raining," Muttknuckles muttered, by way of explanation. "No shortage of guards, though, is there?"

Visceral followed the baron's pointing finger and noticed—for the first time—the army of guards lined up on the hilltop, overlooking the hall. "Great gods," he said. "There must be two hundred of them. I wonder what they're here for."

"I didn't realize Shadewell had a troop contingent," said Curfew, ordering his coach to a halt as the group came upon the village hall.

"Neither did I," said Visceral. "With that many troops, they could probably try for Crust, or Shinbone."

"Or Sneeze," Muttknuckles suggested hopefully.

"Of course," Visceral muttered doubtfully, "that's assuming they belong to Shadewell."

"They're certainly not Modeset's men," Curfew observed, suddenly glad that his city was half a continent away. "Maybe he borrowed them from King Phew. Let's ask him, shall we?"

The other two lords dismounted and passed their respective steeds over to the village's somber-faced stable boys. Prince Blood was already waiting for them, clapping his hands together in order to keep warm.

All four lords were about to head inside, when a loud, booming voice echoed through the village's single street.

"OI!"

The lords turned, as one.

There were four distinct figures standing in the middle of the street. Evidently, they had waited for the lords to pass before strolling out behind them.

Viscount Curfew was the first to step forward. The other lords fanned out behind him, Blood drawing a dagger, Visceral mustering a fireball between his hands, and Muttknuckles sliding a cudgel from the sleeve of his overcoat.

When they were still a good way from the party, which appeared to consist of a normal-sized man, two giants, and a dwarf, they stopped. This was because the first man had marched forward and unfurled a scroll, his irregular companions keeping their distance.

Curfew's breath turned to steam in the air as he waited for the man to speak. There were various mutterings from the other lords as they recognized Pegrand Marshall.

"The following statement," Pegrand began, "has been prepared by the King of Phlegm and his associates. It has also been agreed upon and signed by the newly appointed Duke of Fogrise (that's me, by the way), and ratified by the Captain of the Phlegmian Guard and Overall Commander of the combined Phlegmian/Fogrise alliance. We hereby declare that we wish to remove ourselves from the Great Assembly. We would also like to notify you that, unless you promise faithfully never to interfere in the running of our kingdom, we will be declaring WAR on you in the name of Rackentirin, God of Terrible Carnage, and Mistymeaner, God of Unsuppressed Rage."

There was a moment of silence as everyone waited for Pegrand to recoil the scroll, which he dropped twice.

Finally, Viscount Curfew spoke.

"What is the meaning of this?" he asked, looking at the back of his hands in a distracted manner. "What exactly are you trying to pull, here? There is no *Phlegmian/Fogrise* alliance. Fogrise is a rural district, for goodness' sake. If this is some stupid scheme of Modeset's to get him back into power, it won't work. . . ."

The group went into a huddle before Pegrand emerged once again, unfurling the scroll in his hands.

"The following statement—" he began.

Curfew clapped his hands. "Yes, yes! We got all that, thank you. Where is my cousin?"

Pegrand looked down at his feet. "Duke Modeset is no more."

Behind him, one of the indistinct figures raised

a hand, causing the first line of soldiers on the hill to ready their crossbows.

The lords made a concerted effort to ignore them.

"What about King Phew?" Visceral demanded, emerging from behind Curfew with a fully formed fireball in his hands. "You've killed him, too?"

"We haven't killed *anyone*, yet," Pegrand assured them. "However, unless you agree to our demands, we can't make any promises. . . ."

"Why would we agree to a pathetic treatise written and enforced by morons? Who are those skulkers behind you, anyway?"

Pegrand squinted at the Viscount. "I'm sorry," he said. "But did you just call Groan Teethgrit a moron?"

"Groan Teethgrit is DEAD!" Visceral screamed. "We had assurances from Modeset; he died at the hands of Count Cra—"

A sudden, terrible silence descended on the lords as Groan and Gape stepped into full view, their swords drawn. Gordo was the last to move forward, his battle-axe raised high above his head.

Groan spoke. "Are you agreein' or not?"

"I—" Curfew suddenly trailed off, looking to his

peers for support and finding none. He took a step back, just as three arrows thudded into the patch of ground on which he'd been standing.

The sudden attack had a dramatic effect on the lords. Muttknuckles quickly sleeved his cudgel and shuffled into the background. Prince Blood did likewise, pocketing his knife as he retreated.

Only Earl Visceral stood fast. Being a necromancer of some renown, he had less to fear than the others, and had forged a psychic link with his guard captain. However, he was also a master tactician, and he suspected that even the combined might of the nearby Dullitch-Spittalian troop squads—assuming they agreed to fight together in the first place—would be hard-pressed to match the armed host that amassed on the hills around them. A confrontation, it seemed, would be very unwise.

"Let me get this straight," he snarled instead, eyeing the giant barbarian carefully. "You want us to allow Phlegm *out* of the Great Assembly, in return for which you're offering *what*?"

Groan hefted his broadsword. "I ain't offerin' you nuffin' sept the sharp end o' this sword," he boomed.

"Really," Visceral muttered. "It'll be interesting

to see if you manage to let go of it by the time I've fried your skull with this fireball."

"NO MORE LOOTING," Gordo shouted.

Everyone stared at him, even Groan.

"NO PILLAGING," the dwarf went on. "NO CARAVANS OVERTURNED, NO MERCHANTS ATTACKED. YOU LET US RUN PHLEGM WITHOUT INTERFERENCE, WE LEAVE YOUR CITIES ALONE. FOREVER."

Visceral pursed his lips, then shrugged and dissolved the fireball between his hands. After consulting with the other lords, he stood aside for Viscount Curfew.

"What about trade?" Curfew asked. "We trade regularly with Phlegm."

"Trade continues as normal," said Gape, who'd appointed himself Phlegm's first official chief of the trade industry.

"Yeah," said Groan, who was beginning to feel out of his depth. "An' you all 'ave to call me King Groan, right?"

The earl and Viscount Curfew exchanged glances. Curfew's glance said *this might work to our advantage*, while Visceral's said *there's no "might" about it.*

Prince Blood was thinking along the same

lines, but his attempted discussion with Baron Muttknuckles ended abruptly when the baron blatantly stole some change he'd secreted in a back pocket.

At length, Curfew and Visceral emerged from the fray.

"Agreed," said the Viscount. "You may consider Phlegm removed from the Great Assembly, King Groan. We look forward to much profitable trade with you."

Groan nodded, and began to back away. His generals followed him.

Visceral noticed that, as the Phlegmian quartet disappeared into the distance, the armies on the surrounding hills slowly began to withdraw.

Eventually, the lords of Dullitch, Legrash, Spittle, and Shinbone were alone.

"Well, I certainly didn't expect that," Curfew said, suddenly feeling the cold again.

"Me neither," said Prince Blood. "Still, I never liked Phew that much."

"Agreed," said Curfew. "He didn't trade with us at all, did he?"

"Not once," said Visceral, with a wry smile.

"He traded with me every fortnight," spat

Muttknuckles, stomping toward his donkey. "See? I've bloody lost out again, haven't I?" He clambered awkwardly onto his mule and urged it into a reluctant trot.

"I'm assuming Dullitch'll hold the usual state funeral for Modeset?" he asked, peering over one shoulder.

"Of course," Curfew said, noticing a sudden sly smile from the earl.

"You'll invite the new monarch of Phlegm, I take it?" Visceral muttered.

"Naturally. It'll be a good opportunity to . . . get to know him."

"I'll see you at the funeral, then," shouted Muttknuckles. "If you're all still alive. Ha-ha-ha-ha!"

Curfew watched the baron's tired and inevitably slow departure. Then he turned to his fellow lords and said: "Remind me again why we put up with him?"

EPILOGUE

THE OFFICIAL FUNERAL of Duke Modeset took place one year after the noble's death, partly because no one wanted to host the event and partly because the Phlegmian authorities had failed to find a body in the keep's shark-infested moat. Still, it was a grand affair, attended by lords and ladies from all over Illmoor. The continent's noble elite crowded atop the Dullitch tor, jostling for position among the newly elected rulers of Phlegm, Spittle, Sneeze, and Legrash. Groan Teethgrit, the King of Phlegm, was not present, having recently enjoyed the birth of his first son.

But that, as they say, is another story. . . .

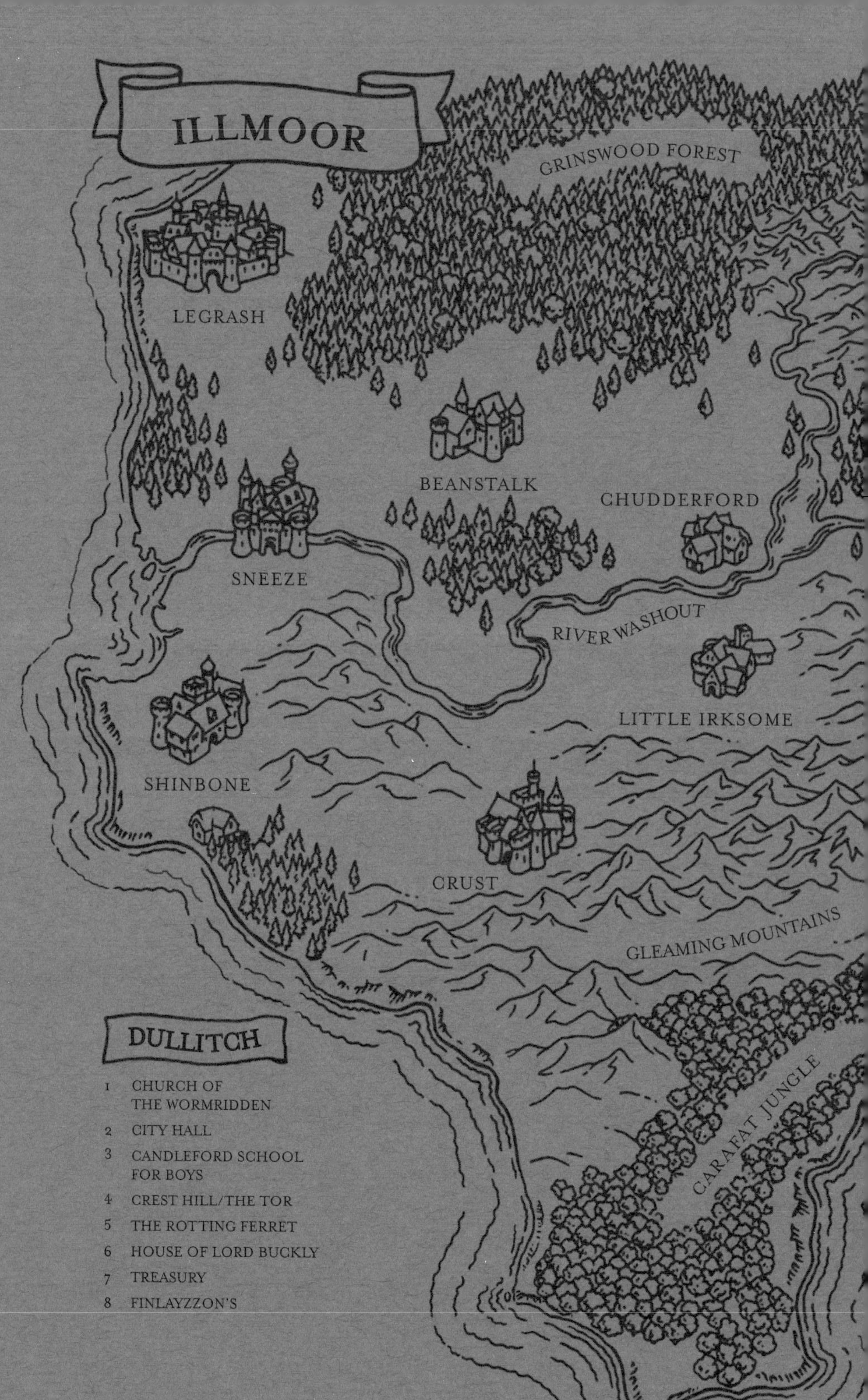
ILLMOOR
GRINSWOOD FOREST
LEGRASH
BEANSTALK
CHUDDERFORD
SNEEZE
RIVER WASHOUT
LITTLE IRKSOME
SHINBONE
CRUST
GLEAMING MOUNTAINS
CARAFAT JUNGLE
DULLITCH
1 CHURCH OF THE WORMRIDDEN
2 CITY HALL
3 CANDLEFORD SCHOOL FOR BOYS
4 CREST HILL/THE TOR
5 THE ROTTING FERRET
6 HOUSE OF LORD BUCKLY
7 TREASURY
8 FINLAYZZON'S